The House of Curtains

by G. H. Teed

Illustrated by Eric Parker

First published in the Sexton Blake Library,
Series 2, No 293, 2 July 1931.

Stillwoods Edition

Stillwoods.Blogspot.Ca

Catalogue Information:
Title: The House of Curtains
Author: G. H. Teed (1881-1938)
Illustrated by: Eric Parker
First published in the Sexton Blake Library, Series 2, No 293, 2 July 1931.
This Edition by: Stillwoods, 2021, (Doug Frizzle)
ISBN Canada: 978-1-989788-72-1
Blog: Stillwoods.Blogspot.Ca
Author Blog: http://ghteed.blogspot.com/
Storefront: http://www.lulu.com
Copyright © Doug Frizzle and/or Stillwoods, 2021.
Cover adapted from the original.

Keywords: Sexton Blake, British fictional detective, Tinker

https://tinyurl.com/ve25d42s This link should go to a spreadsheet of all known Teed stories. The list is annotated with various information on the stories and my progress with recapturing the work. The library of Teed's stories increases almost weekly. Check at the **Lulu.Com** for the latest arrivals. Search for Teed./drf

Cautionary Note: This series of books by Stillwoods are intended to make the stories of G. H. Teed, born in New Brunswick, Canada, available to collectors and researchers. The editor, or rather digitizer has not altered the original publication.

This story may contain language and racial terms that are not appropriate to today. I apologize for them; I know that the author was using his voice to excite and entertain an adventurous English audience. These works were published from 82 to 110 years ago. Most every work has characters of redeeming ethnicity within.

I hope you enjoy and share these stories; I have.
Doug Frizzle

THE HOUSE OF CURTAINS

Notes:

Hodder reports this as repeated in Detective Weekly 1939, as 'The Island of Lost Men'.

Wondering if it might also have been published, 'de-Blaked,' as a hardcover...

Hopefully, just temporarily, the Blakiana website is down. It provides the best information on all materials relating to Sexton Blake. It is a creation of Mark Hodder.

/drf

Amazing Drama of Sinister Mystery Abroad.

The Leading Detective-Story Magazine.

Four new volumes of the Sexton Blake Library are issued on the first Thursday of next month. Order them Now!

An amazing long complete novel of detective adventure abroad.

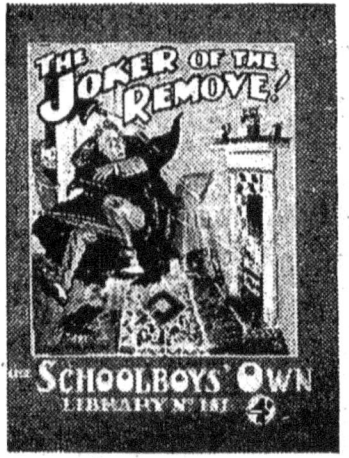

Chapter 1.   The Man Who Wouldn't Squeal.

STEFAN GOUPOLIS, overlord of the lovely little island of Mitkos in the Ægean Sea, sat at his ease on the broad, colonnaded piazza of his villa, gazing out over the slopes of intense green that stretched to the very edge of the blue, blue water.

The green was that of almonds and olives, of roses and tender shrubs that had been born under the caress of the soft Levantine breezes. For Mitkos was one of the classic isles of Greece.

At least, that was how it was generally regarded, but its exact status was one of considerable doubt and confusion. It lay practically on the imaginary line that bounded the Dodecanese Archipelago that extends from the eastern tip of Crete to the coast of Asia Minor, and, therefore, might be —as it is by some —regarded as under Italian sovereignty.

On the other hand, a more recent survey of the boundaries of the Dodecanese since the great Greek debacle of 1926 has revealed some doubt as to whether the line passes south of Mitkos, through it, or to the north. If the former, it would indisputably belong to Greece; if the latter, then it would come into the Italian group; and if neither, if the line actually crossed it, then it would be a bone of contention between the two nations.

If either thought it worth while to fight over. As a matter of fact, the papers relating to the different claims were still going the rounds of various governmental departments in both countries, gathering a little more weight of red-tape and a little more grubbiness as the months and years passed. It seemed that neither country was anxious to press the claim to a point where unpleasantness might develop — and for a very good reason.

Mitkos was far too small and unimportant to quarrel over. Its total circumference would not be more than five or six miles; its population was but a handful; its products only the trifling harvest that came off the estate of the overlord, Stefan Goupolis.

It had been under the feudal control of the Goupolis family for many generations. When it had come under Grecian claim with no one to dispute, it had been left strictly alone, for the simple reason that the overlords were easily angered, and strenuously opposed the intrusion of outsiders.

The present overlord had exhibited the same temper when the

Italians would have landed an agent on the island, and, for some reason best known to themselves, they had quickly withdrawn the irritant.

Since then Stefan Goupolis had been left entirely alone to rule his tiny domain as he saw fit. Nor did either country exact tribute from him.

Truth to tell, the place seemed quite too trifling to worry about. Yet Stefan Goupolis was accounted a very rich man even among the rich Greek merchants of Athens and Smyrna and Alexandria.

His villa was a wonderful residence of white marble, built on a terrace overlooking the sea. Its classic lines were as graceful as those of any temple of ancient Greece, its interior furnishings and decorations of exquisite choice in design and beauty of execution.

His private yacht, that rode in a sheltered little bay, had cost close to a million in England; his smaller craft, three of them, one a sixty-foot speed-boat, one a cabined cruiser, and the other a Bermuda-rigged schooner, were other toys of a rich man. His great marble swimming-bath was something that the most sensuous film-star would have envied.

And there were bath-rooms galore in the villa, a private ice-making plant, a small, beautiful theatre, gardens, arbours of green foliage on the flat roof, a tiny stream that had been turned to a dozen different uses, even a private riding circuit that went right round the little island and carried through it in different directions, so that one could choose a different way every day.

Then, secluded in another grove by the sea, were his people —the peasants who tilled his soil, the sturdy, brown-skinned sailors who manned his different craft, his employees of higher grade, the women and brown children, the wide, airy stables, and, by no means least, a very powerful wireless sending and receiving station.

Within itself Mitkos was a miniature world where its inhabitants could complete the whole cycle of life, of love, of passion and hate, of good and evil, without depending for a single grain upon the outer abodes of mankind. It could exist, were it necessary, as complete a unit as if it were a minor planet riding alone in the cosmos.

The interior of the villa was so extensive as to be almost vast. Pillared from front to back as the wide piazza was colonnaded, it was like the court of a Greek temple. But that was but a small portion of the chamber arrangement; and nothing at all of the immensity of the mystery and secrecy of Villa Mitkos that was known only to the reigning overlord of the island.

While it is a fact that substantial wealth had come down to Stefan Goupolis from his father and grandfather, his inheritance had not been sufficient to cover more than a tithe of his expenditure.

The estate paid its upkeep, but little more. It did not begin to yield him a profit to indulge in all the luxuries which surrounded him. And his annual expenditure was enormous.

Then whence came the money for yachts and thoroughbred horses, for the amazing bacchanalian revels in which he periodically indulged, bringing his guests across from Athens or Alexandria and entertaining them for days at prodigious expense?

Where did he draw on for the money that purchased the jewels he showered on his women friends? Whence came it for the rare books and pictures and statuary? Into what chest did he dig to keep the great steam yacht, a miniature ocean liner, the lovely sailing yacht, the long speed-boat that ate money?

Yet money flowed like water through his hands. Thousands upon thousands would he pitch away without a thought. And, always, there scorned plenty more to draw on.

Whence?

In Athens and in Smyrna it was whispered that Stefan Goupolis had made many millions during the Great War smuggling arms to the Greeks. In Alexandria it was told that he had cleaned up millions at the time of the Greek debacle in Smyrna when the Turks drove the fleeting Greeks into the sea. In London and in Paris, in the great financial centres it was said that the paper of Stefan Goupolis was good for any sum. But in none of those places was the real truth guessed.

In Odessa, in the Russian Ukraine, however, in Bombay, Marseilles, and many other ports right along up the China coast as far as Shanghai, a certain coterie of persons knew that Stefan Goupolis on his island of Mitkos was one of the most important links in the chain which connects up the vast ramifications of the illicit drug traffic against which almost every nation and the League of Nations are impotent.

Lying as it does in the eastern Mediterranean, Mitkos occupies a strategic position which it would be difficult to improve upon. It is within easy distance of the main lane through which all the sea traffic passes from one end to the other of the great inland seas; it commands the approach to Constantinople and the Black Sea, with all Russia beyond; it is an ideal junction for surreptitious landings and transfers from ships bound to or from Marseilles or Port Said and beyond. It is the drug cross-roads, so to say, of the whole terrific organisation, and Stefan Goupolis is its keeper.

Hence his millions and multi-millions.

It is not to be taken that Stefan Goupolis had continued to occupy such a position of power without there having arisen many, at different times, to challenge him. But, quite aside from his indisputable ownership of the island, his influence was such and his power accepted so in those places that counted in Greece, Italy and Turkey, that, no matter what national squabbles might be in progress, Goupolis on his island was let alone.

Nor was he unprepared for attack. While, outwardly, the Villa Mitkos revealed no signs of defence, it would have been found, had an attack been opened, that both villa and island were fairly bristling with heavy pieces and machine-guns, and that there were plenty of qualified men to handle them. There were, too, in an underground hangar that was perfectly concealed and opened to a wide, flat take-off by a very gentle slope, three aeroplanes, two fighting bombers, and a cruising 'plane with a non-landing radius of something over a thousand miles.

It is little wonder, therefore, that Stefan Goupolis should survey his domain with a good deal of content on this warm afternoon as he sat smoking and gazing out over the blue Ægean that stretched away to the Cyclades, while, from the hidden village came faint sounds of the hammering and other activities of his people. He was king, and this was his kingdom.

And none within that kingdom disputed his authority. It was utter, even unto that or life and death.

It was not often that his hospitality was extended to guests. Three or four times each year he would fill his yacht with men and women and bring them back from Egypt or the Riviera or Spain. And for a week or so, the orgies would continue.

Then he would ship them away again, and for weeks to come would live the life of a hermit, an ascetic.

It was during one of these lone periods that he sat on the broad piazza smoking while the life of the island hummed about him. On a table, close at hand, were cigarettes and coffee, in his lap a sheaf of typed papers, the news of the outside world which was collected each day through his private wireless and prepared for his perusal.

He was as well informed hourly as if he lived in London, Paris, New York, Berlin, or any other great centre. He knew the fluctuations of the share and money market to a fraction; he followed the doings of governments with a cynical amusement; he took toll, twice daily, of world commodity prices.

From his retreat he could speculate on any exchange or bourse in the world. His credits were well spread out so that cover for his transactions was always ready.

But on this particular afternoon he was not thinking of such things. He was pondering on an incident that had developed to a point that must be scored off at exactly four o'clock.

Three days before a man had been caught prowling about the villa in the early hours of the morning. He had been hauled before the overlord by the two guards who had discovered him, and had been identified as a fellow who had joined the crew of the Bermuda-rigged schooner some months before when she had put in at Messina in Sicily for certain supplies that were wanted on the island.

Until this incident no suspicion had been roused against him. He had claimed to be, and had appeared to be, an ordinary Sicilian sailor. His record was good enough until this display of curiosity regarding the interior of the villa.

But since then, through means which were used on Mitkos as they had been used by the Turks in years gone, by —that is, the bastinado —certain, admissions had been wrung from the tortured creature's lips.

These admissions had been enough to veil Stefan Goupolis that he was a spy, and one of considerable importance. He had taken this means of reaching Mitkos to discover what he could of its secret.

Goupolis knew perfectly well that a very large reward was ready for the one who could reveal the secret of the underground drug traffic that controlled world supplies. He knew that every country subscribing to the League of Nations would be glad to contribute towards the amount of such reward.

To get under the crust of the main tunnel, so to say, was a very different thing from nabbing petty peddlers in different cities. It was the source of the stuff which the League was after, not the small distributors.

Time and again they had proved themselves helpless. There was the clearing of the cargo of opium and morphia a few months back from Odessa that had been done openly. It had been spoken of in the League meeting at Geneva. Yet none of the world powers or smaller countries had been able to lift a finger to stop it. Many weeks after it had been reported off the China Coast, its cargo gone.

And a wave of laughter had passed all the way from Odessa to Shanghai and from Marseilles to Bombay, finding a lodging place on the island of Mitkos as it passed.

Again, another cargo of morphine and its various derivatives such as heroin and so on, had been shipped from a Persian port. What had become of it no one knew. But weeks after, that same ship had been spotted in a Spanish port unloading coal.

The network was impenetrable; the web so vast that it seemed no single key knot could be loosed.

The arrival of this spy from Messina was the nearest that anyone had succeeded in getting towards the main channel. And, more than once during the past two days, Stefan Goupolis had debated within himself just what fate he should deal out to the impertinent fellow.

He had reported the discovery in secret code through his wireless. He had received in reply, many more code messages which tended but to confirm that the fellow must be a spy acting for the League of Nations.

After the first few admissions even the bastinado had failed to drag anything more from the lips of the tortured man. And Stefan Goupolis was not one to waste time when he had satisfied himself of what he wanted to know.

At four o'clock, he had given orders that the man was to be brought to the courtyard at the back where he was accustomed to judge misdemeanors. Very well, at four o'clock he would be on his stone seat ready to pass sentence.

When his wrist watch showed him it was two minutes to four he rose, a frail figure with spindle shanks showing as the breeze laid the silk legs of his trousers flat. In age he might have been anything between thirty and fifty. As a matter of fact, he was just thirty-seven though, the transparent, tightly drawn sallow skin of his face was criss-crossed with thousands of minute wrinkles. His eyes were dark, steady, very intelligent. His nose was long thin, straight; his mouth, a bitter, mocking slit. A thin gold-headed, ebony cane lay against the comfortable wicker long chair in which it had been lounging, but instead of picking it up he caught hold of two walnut-sized spheres of beautiful amber which, were connected by a silken cord about nine inches long. These he began to twist about in his left hand as he walked, twisting and turning and rubbing as one sees them throughout the Balkans until the heated amber sends soothing electric currents up along the arm to the brain.

He walked through the spacious, beautifully proportioned pillared hall and came out on to the back piazza which faced on a green patio in the centre of which was a tinkling fountain. On the far side of this was a heavy gate of carved mahogany which had once adorned a noble Spanish casa, but which had been looted originally by the invading Moors. How it had found its way to Mitkos those centuries ago only the records of the dead and gone Goupolis of the time could have told.

Two white-coated, black-skinned Nubians appeared as if from nowhere and opened the gate for his passage. He stepped immediately into another courtyard, stone cobbled, with aged moss growing between the polished roundness of the stones. Under a pillared stone canopy was a wide, stone seat set on a low dais, and into this the overlord slid his thin body, looking almost childish in contrast with the massive carved flutings of the stone.

Somewhere a bell tolled four. At once, another gate opened into the court and a small file of white-uniformed men entered. Two were in front, two next, with a handcuffed wretch between them, and two behind. First and last couples were armed with cutlasses and rifles; the middle pair wore heavy service revolvers from the belt and each carried a cutless over his shoulder.

They advanced, without any officer to wheel before the stone seat and come into line so that the prisoner stood directly before the judge.

He wasted no time. Speaking in French he addressed the man who cringed before him.

"You are ready to speak now?"

"I have told all I know, monsieur."

"That, of course, is a lie," remarked Goupolis equably. "I have had my warning conveyed to you. I never change my mind. If you will lay before me full information as to why you came and what you hoped to discover I am prepared to deal leniently with you. At worst I

7

shall have your tongue cut out and keep you prisoner on the island. If you refuse you die within the hour."

"I have nothing to say, monsieur."

"One more chance —will you speak?"

"No —curses on you for a dog of evil. I have done my duty. I have failed. Others will come after me and dig out this nest of yours. And if they fail there will be still others, for this drug game is doomed."

Stefan Goupolis smiled slightly.

"You have spoken at last," he said softly. "Be it so. We shall take good care that you at least, tell nothing. It is finished. Take him to the Grotto."

As he finished speaking the six guards fell into twos again, the prisoner being dragged away by force since he seemed unwilling to walk. They vanished as they had come, the big gate slammed, then the overlord rose languidly and returned to the villa —a noble white palace lying against the intense green beneath the afternoon sun that should have been a temple of beauty, but which, instead, was a naked mausoleum of brooding horror.

Chapter 2.   The Grotto of Horror.

WITHIN the pillared hall Stefan Goupolis turned and approached a fretted stone panel that had been set in the northern wall.

The carving was lacy and as exquisite as the facade of Rouen Cathedral. Yet it must have been of very modern workmanship for, when the man pressed a spot in what appeared to be solid marble, the whole panel opened smoothly and silently, revealing a small lift.

Goupolis stepped inside and the panel closed after him. Then he touched a button that caused the lift to descend. When it came to rest, he caused another panel to open and emerged into a place that was in startling contrast to the sun-washed surface above.

Above him rose a series of arches, each pendant with miniature forests of stalactites. On all sides were black, smooth walls, dripping with moisture that collected in little pools before overflowing into a silent, ebony stream that disappeared through the grottos.

In among the frosty daggers, many pale blue lights had been fixed so that the place was shrouded in a ghostly glow of blue, that was lessened by the salty whiteness of the stalactites.

Along the side of the stream where Goupolis stood, was a smooth walkway, and now the overlord began to follow its course.

Through grotto after grotto he went, each one almost a replica of the other, until, ahead of him, the light became pure white. Then he emerged into a large round chamber that was filled with an exquisite pearly glow.

It was an extraordinary place. The roof was of glass, over which lay a carpet of limpid water. On every side, through the thick plate glass one could see the lovely colouring of a sea garden with fish of exotic colours swimming lazily among the fronds. Strange to say, no sea lichen or barnacles clung to the surface of the dome, but that was because divers descended regularly to keep it clear. As a matter of fact, as much attention was given to this marine garden as to the terraced stretches above ground.

The atmosphere of the place was almost tropical. Within the walls were a profusion of palms and orchids and, round the circular walls were glass-fronted cases filled with books. Couches, easy wicker chairs, tables, vividly-coloured rugs —a retreat such as any lover of quiet and beauty might envy.

But even this bower of loveliness possessed its poison fang.

In the centre of the place was, what appeared to be a heavy glass plate about ten feet in diameter. Standing close to it one could see the limpid black water from the stream, it flowed beneath, finding its way into the sea through some invisible opening. It was like standing above a sheeted pool of ink.

But when Goupolis touched a button that was set in one of the marble pillars that ringed the space, a brilliant white light burst forth beneath, and now one could see coral white rocks far down with, as a carpet, snowy sand.

Then the horror appeared.

Out from a small grotto formed by a group of the coral-white stones, emerged something long and black, and slimy, groping, feeling, stretched towards the brilliance of the light above.

It came, it lengthened as if it were uncoiling from a birth-head that was fashioning it even as was thrust forth.

As it writhed like a snake, the watching man could see that the tip was puckered into horrible lips and the paler underside spaced with other, smaller puckers that opened and closed like suckers.

A second tentacle followed the first, writhing like its fellow. It lengthened even more monstrously as it lifted to the very glass of the plate on which the man stood gazing down.

The end lips touched the plate and at once clung to it with powerful suction.

The tentacle was now close beside it and, peering down between them, Goupolis could make out something terribly evil in the opening to the grotto —a purplish, squat mass with a horrible orifice slit in it that gaped inky black.

It was a giant squid, beside which the octopus is a thing of beauty. It was one of those terrible sea squids, such as are to be found among the islands of the West Indies and from one of those deserted bays had it been brought in a tank to this subterranean pool on the island of Mitkos.

Goupolis tapped his foot on the thick glass just over the spot where one of the tentacles suctioned. A quiver ran down the whole length of the horrid feeler, communicating itself to the other. The mass in the opening seemed to become excited in a gross, sluggish way. It emerged still farther until, one might think it possible to distinguish a repulsive organ of sight set in the fleshy folds; but one could not be sure.

All this time Goupolis had been rubbing and frictioning the amber spheres in his left hand, and now they were revolving as fast as his fingers could turn them, only visible proof that the man was in the throes of some ghastly excitement.

Suddenly he straightened up and, reaching once more towards the nearest marble pillar, pressed another button. Nothing visible or audible occurred here in the garden room, but he knew that, beyond the walls a bell had rung.

The response was almost immediate. Scarcely had he turned back to peer down into the pool than, so directly beneath that edge he could not see it, a panel shot open and a naked human figure was precipitated into the writhing clutches of the squid.

Goupolis had one fleeting glimpse of the horror-stricken face of the spy he had condemned; saw the paleness of the human body twisting and turning in the eager folds of the squid's tentacles; watched a stream of air bubbles shoot up to the surface and cling to the glass on which he stood; then the whole interior of the pool was filled with an inky cloud that suffused every portion of the water, blotted out the white of rocks and sand, enfolded the scene in a swirling chaos of unseen movement that seemed to thicken and thicken until it became almost like jelly.

Then stillness.

Goupolis shrugged his shoulders and switched out the light that had become a futile thing. Humming lightly to himself, he strolled about the marine room, admiring his orchids, peering through the thick plate glass appreciatively at the loveliness beyond. Even when the sun did not penetrate to light his garden, he could throw it into an even greater loveliness by means of powerful arc lights that could be switched on from within.

But he had another purpose in coming down here on this occasion. When he reached a certain place on the eastern side of the great room, he paused to press the control switch of a huge steel door that was cunningly concealed by a close-growing tropical ivy.

Another switch gave illumination of a large shed-like place into which he stepped. And here he walked slowly round the shape of what any naval man would have recognised as a small, but very modern submarine craft.

A few feet beyond its shapely nose were huge, double steel doors that could be opened to admit the inrush of the sea. It was, in fact, a dry-dock that could be flooded at will, either from outside or inside the submarine and it gave Stefan Goupolis just one other means of safeguard and escape.

The craft was creature of his own brain. It gave him a peculiar delight to walk about it and study its smooth lines, to lay his hand, on its cool steel plates, to visualise it cutting through the depths as swiftly and as certainly as a killer shark.

When he had completed his tour of inspection, he returned to the door that communicated with the marine room. Yet even now he could not scorn to take his eyes from the submarine, for he turned to gaze at it again and, as he did so, he murmured:

"Lovely, lovely —they know naught of you, my beauty. Let them try to ferret out the secret Mitkos. Let them send whom they will. I am ready. You are one link in the chain, my beauty, that remains my own secret. Preparedness is strength and Stefan Goupolis is prepared."

He spoke truly enough. He was prepared. He was strong. He had guarded at every point where his armour might show a chink. He had riches untold to buy men to do his bidding. He had planned every step of any possible flight he might have to make. It mattered not to him whither he might be driven. He had plenty of money stored in a score of different cities in a dozen different countries.

Impregnable.

Was he? In London there was a man who believed that no armour ever was forged, but had its chink. He was even then beginning to move against the stronghold of Mitkos.

That man was Sexton Blake.

Chapter 3.   The Dope Victim.

THE trail started in London.

A girl had hysterics in a Soho den. A French Senegalese negro throttled her screams into silence. The girl's Italian lover stabbed the negro in the back before the lights went out.

The whole mob of riff-raff, white women, half-caste women, black men, yellow men, and what-not rushed the stairs that led to the street.

They arrived at the top just in time to be met by a squad of police, who had planned the raid long ago, and had timed their visit perfectly.

Into the wreckage of the den went Detective-inspector Thomas, of Scotland Yard, with a sergeant and two constables. With him were Sexton Blake and his young assistant, Tinker.

Cowering in the dark office was the patron of the place. They gathered him in easily enough, and, after serving a term, he would be deported.

On the floor, however, they found something more worthy of their attention— the negro who had been stabbed, and the girl whom he had tried to strangle.

The black was dead, the knife still stuck between his ribs. The girl was moaning. Saliva was dropping from the corner of her mouth. Her thin dress was in ribbons; her hair was sticky with drink and ashes where her head rested on the floor.

At the earnest request of Sexton Blake permission was given for the girl to be taken to a nursing-home only two doors from his own house at Baker Street.

Blake asked his friend and personal physician, Dr. McKenzie, of Devonshire Street, to see the girl. It was soon obvious to that experienced medico that the girl was not suffering chiefly from the throat pressure she had undergone. The knife had plunged into her assailant's heart before her life had been endangered.

What he did find was a pronounced drug case, and that he set himself to treat. It was a stiff fight. The girl was in a state of acute hysteria that broke out again and again as the days and nights passed. It was necessary to bring her along carefully by administering more drug at intermittent periods, but, gradually, the quantum was lessened until her system was purged of the stuff, if her nerves were still jumpy from the effects.

Had she been addicted to the habit for a considerable time, she would not have responded so readily. But she was young, and, although it was obvious that she had been doping heavily, eating little, smoking and drinking much, she retained enough constitution unimpaired to build on.

For three weeks Sexton Blake visited her daily, talking with her when she seemed inclined to listen, but never mentioning the affair at the den in Soho.

With improvement in health came a marvellous alteration in her appearance. She developed a smile in place of the sulky expression she had worn. Her lips changed from bloodless, puffy pads to rich red. Her eyes acquired lustre; her whole skin toned altogether to a remarkable degree.

She had been pretty before she plunged into the hectic life; she was pretty again.

It was not until she herself chose to speak of the affair that Blake touched on the subject. Even then he brushed it aside as something not to be dwelt upon at length. But he led her along gently until he knew as much as she could tell him.

Her evidence, taken on commission, was admitted to the trial of the Italian who had stabbed the black. It was that evidence, plus what Sexton Blake had to say, that was responsible for the Italian getting no more than ten years on a conviction of justifiable homicide.

The police did not press the case too hard. It was known that weightier matters lay behind it all, and they, like Sexton Blake, were only too anxious to probe the mystery.

Blake was allowed to see the Italian just before he was taken away to begin his sentence. He handed him a long letter from the girl in the nursing-home, and waited while he read it. But he was ready for the question which he knew the other would ask.

"What do you want to know?"

"I'll tell you when you answer some other questions. You owe a lot to that girl, as you must acknowledge."

"Let it go at that."

"We will not. There are other things. You would have been a good case for hanging if it had not been for her evidence —and mine. The police have not been vindictive to you. Nor will they question you as I shall —in a private capacity. At the very least, it would have been a 'lifer' for you. But you have got off with ten years, which means, with allowances, no more than a little over seven. That isn't so much for a fellow of your age."

"That nigger deserved it. He would have killed her."

"Maybe so. But there is little choice among any of you who were in that den that night. You may be a number when you are in prison, but you won't be out of mind of several persons. Better to have me as a friend outside than to have none."

"What do you want to know?"

"Where you got it."

"Got —what? I don't understand you."

"Don't quibble. You know how you made a living. The girl has told me enough. I've discovered quite a lot more. I know that you handled enough of the stuff to rank as a chief agent for big interests. You got it direct from abroad. I'm not interested in knowing how you smuggled it into this country. I only want to know what source it came from."

"That wouldn't do you any good."

"I'm the best judge of that. Will you tell me?"

"They would 'get' me when I came out."

"I'll stand by you. They won't be active in another seven years. Spill me this information, and I'll see that you get a start when you come out."

Thus it went on for the better part of two hours, the Italian constantly hedging, the detective persuading by every possible argument. And, at last, he went away with a name.

That name took him to Belgium. From Belgium he followed the faint, faint trail to Switzerland. From Switzerland he went to Genoa; from that great Italian port he moved cautiously along the French Riviera until certain information sent him hotfoot to Barcelona. He was scarcely in Barcelona before he started back for Marseilles —a hint in his possession that might mean anything; and if it led him to something definite it would lead him, too, as he well realised, into the very jaws of the tiger men.

And with him, all through that pilgrimage, went Tinker.

Sexton Blake knew perfectly well that, so far he was barely tugging at one tiny end of a stray cord that might be linked up with the main net that was cast over most of the civilised globe.

But that was enough for the present. He knew that the interlacings of this same net drew in its booty from places as far apart as Buenos Aires and Shanghai, as Valparaiso and Yokohama, as Melbourne and London, as New York and Calcutta, as Capetown and Montreal.

He knew the ramifications of the system crossed and criss-crossed even more bewilderingly than that of the white-slave traffic; yet he knew, too, that they touched with common interest at more than one point.

The shrewdest spies of a dozen nations had tried to penetrate that web, had even allowed themselves to become a unit in it to try and trace the maze to its source, without result other than to disappear.

Yet it groaned and crawled, and gobbled its victims in their thousands and hundreds of thousands.

Where was the heart of the monster? Where was the one cord that would vibrate to the inner circles of the vast web? Who were the men who drew that net and recast it and drew it again? Were they monsters who lived, unsuspected, in the great cities, engaged, ostensibly, in some perfectly respectable business, honoured, courted? Or did they hide beneath the shadows?

Sexton Blake knew that only extraordinary patience and an entirely original form of investigation would give him a hint of the truth. He knew that instinct would tell him when he was in contact with one of the links of the main chain. But how to creep close enough?

The course he had followed across the Continent of Europe had taught him much about the traffic in general, but it was little more than he had guessed. He knew, however, that he had not yet got past even the outer door of caution, he had been dealing with those who were as ignorant as himself, distributors, agents, and so on, who had no real idea as to how the stuff reached them.

It was only when he reached Barcelona that a faint, faint, whisper reached him. It was so little, so uninformative that it seemed he must be following but another will o' the wisp. But it had sent him on to Marseilles, and, on a certain evening when the rain swept in from the Mediterranean, he and his short, stocky companion, dressed like rough and dirty Catalonian seamen, took their way ashore from a filthy Spanish tramp and plunged into the Thieves' Quarter of Marseilles —as vicious a haunt as is to be found in any seaport in the world.

Not only was Blake dressed as a Catalonian, in extravagantly loose blue breeches, blue jersey, red shirt and a tasselled blue and red cap of tam-o-shanter shape, but he posed as one as well, for he could burr that broad, unpleasing Spanish of that part of the coast like a native.

Tinker, on the other hand, did not profess to be other than a waif of the sea. His speech was mongrel, deliberately made a mixture of French-Canadian, waterside American, Thames-side cockney, Sydney-side Australian and low-class French with a streak of Buenos Aires Spanish.

There were plenty like him to be found among the motley hordes that the sea throws up in the vastness of Marseilles port, or, in fact, in any port where the ships of the world pause.

Their objective in the Thieves' Quarter was quite definite. In Blake's clothes, carefully hidden away in a bit of oiled silk, was a tiny piece of paper on which a word was written. That, he had been given to understand in Barcelona, would be the passport he needed to a certain thing he sought. Though the one who had given him that paper never guessed what purpose lay behind the request. Had he done so Blake would have received a knife in his heart instead.

No one molested them as they got deeper and deeper into the district, though they were already so far away from the lights of the Cannebiere that no police would dare to venture in unless they came in force. It is a quarter which is left strictly alone by the authorities except at those times when the seething cauldron boils over. Then there is a short period of hell popping, after which the stew simmers down again. But always, underneath, the volcano is ready to burst forth.

Blake's present objective was the Green Woman, a place known by repute, at least, to every rover of the seven seas; and that repute was about as vile as possible.

Its history went back a long time, years and years, until no one could rightly say when it had first opened its doors as a wine-shop. Men of the old wind-jammer days had known it and many of them had ventured deeply enough into the quarter to find it.

Steam kettle sailors remained too short a time in port for many of them to penetrate that far; and, besides, of late years, it was a place one left alone.

Its history of crime was black. Yet it was no worse than other dens in the same quarter, that alien district which licked its festering sores and snarled viciously when disturbed.

The Thieves' Quarter, in relation to the rest of the city of Marseilles, lies along the waterfront to the west of the outer basin. A certain part of it has been scooped entirely away by the big dredges that brought the waters of the Rhone Canal right into the inner basin; but that only had the effect of throwing the outer denizens in upon their fellows, congesting the noisesomeness that already strained within taut boundaries.

From its water parallel it rises through chalky cliffs up to the sheer face of a hill beyond which is a wide area of waste ground that divides it from a more respectable quarter.

Its streets are narrow, short, dividing so frequently and so abruptly as to be extremely confusing to the stranger unless he keeps in mind that the slope leads, always, through the tortuous maze to the waterfront. But it is easier to tell that to one's-self than to follow even what should be a direct descent, for an unexpected turning takes one upwards again when it should go down.

From the upper part a portion of the outer basin is visible. One can see, too, the sheer hills that rise as islands in the harbour, the Chateau d'If where the Count of Monte Cristo was imprisoned and from which he escaped, lying against the blue like a blotch of white and ochre-yellow cake. Then, beyond that, the gleaming spire of the Church of the Martyrs.

But these things were not visible on that drenching night when the two Catalonians ploughed their way through the unclean streets and flooded gutters to the Green Woman. Only a few lights showed here and there; only other shadowy figures passed them, bent against the storm.

Their first glimpse of the Green Woman— they both knew it from a previous visit to the quarter —was a pool of light lying on the wet road. It fell from the front window of the wine-shop, and, as they drew nearer, they saw another patch of light in the alley on one side.

Now the sound of maudlin singing reached them, voices of women as well as men. Someone was playing an accordion, and, drawing still nearer, they heard a steady "thump-thump-thumpety-thump" which came from tapping feet. It was evident that, despite, or on account of, the dirty night, the wine-shop was doing good business.

On reaching the half-swing doors Blake did not hesitate. He

knew perfectly well that more than one pair of eyes inside would take note of his feet beneath the bottom of the doors, and that, before he could possibly cross the threshold, as much as they could tell would be read from them.

He hinged against a leaf of the door and lurched in, scowling. Tinker came close at his heels, snapping his hands up and down to shake the worst of the rain from his sleeves. He, too, was scowling, and, in their disguises, with dirty faces, unkempt locks and discoloured teeth, they looked fit addition for the company within.

It was not a large place, though its peculiar arrangement allowed a far greater number of persons inside than one would have thought —from the street —could have been accommodated with comfort.

The main saloon was typical —furnished with iron topped tables and iron-framed chairs. On the right was a zinc-covered bar behind which was the patron, a heavy-jowled, enormous individual with as hard a pair of eyes as were over set in human sockets. His shirt, open at the neck, revealed the top of a thick mat of chest-hair, and one could scarcely see the skin of the arms, so thickly hirsute were they.

He fixed the two newcomers with a stare. In one brief moment he had classed them— so he thought. They looked neither too much of one thing nor too much of another. There were plenty more of the same type in the place, and, as such, they could pass muster. But before they were there very long he would know from which ship they came.

The chairs in the outer saloon were nearly all occupied, a good proportion of the clients being women of the quarter. Through the doors which had been left open into the other room a space had been cleared, and here some couples were dancing a sort of fandango to the tune of the accordion which was being played by an ancient, gnome-like fellow who perched on a table.

Then, to the left, some steps led up to an odd sort of half-room, a waist-high railing acting as a guard to prevent a staggering client from tumbling into the room beneath. It was, as a matter of fact, an extension over the roof of a low building next door, and this it was that took the overflow of the two lower rooms.

Four waiters did duty below and two above, the sextette being as dirty as most of the clients. The male element of these were the general habitues of the quarter with the influx from the ships; the women were regulars, dressing in the way that marked them as such, their dresses very low in the throat, their skirts very short.

Blake and Tinker mounted the steps to the half-floor above. On reaching it they saw in one corner a serving-hatch, in which stood a very stout woman who wore a vivid green dress. She was by no means the original Green Woman of the wine-shop name, but each patronne since the first had made it a custom to wear a dress of that colour.

Her inspection of the newcomers was as swift and thorough as that of her husband; but she had a fat, oily smile for them, where the man had stared woodenly.

Blake made her a bow which Tinker copied. Then he sought a table at one end of the railing from where they could look down into the room beneath.

When the waiter came up he ordered coffee for two, chunks of bread and meat for two and two glasses of beer. The service was primitive enough, the food being served on one plate without either knife or fork. But that was a small detail in the Green Woman, the feeding implement being one's clasp knife. And Blake and Tinker used each his ship's knife as adeptly as any of the others.

So far, so good. Blake had covered another stride on the long, difficult journey he had set himself. But he knew that, did he fail to achieve his purpose here, he must go back the whole way and try to make a fresh start. His fate in the Green Woman rested entirely on the efficacy of that tiny piece of paper which was hidden in his clothing.

Chapter 4.   The Password.

IT was the woman in green to whom Blake must give his bit of paper.

But he knew the time was not yet. It would be necessary to wait until he had established himself, so to speak. There were still many odd, furtive glances being cast towards him and Tinker. They were strangers and, as such, would be suspect until something diverted attention from them.

That diversion came sooner than he expected.

It began with high voices in the inner saloon. The music kept on for a bit but, peering over the rail, Blake and Tinker could see that the dancing had stopped.

The women had fled to one end of the room, where they were huddled against the wall, their eyes fixed on a tableau which, for the moment, was hidden from Blake and the lad.

The crowd immediately beneath them had risen and was pressing towards the open door; the clients on the upper floor where they eat were packing down the stairs to get a better view.

Then, over the heads of the press, Blake saw two figures come circling slowly into the line of vision.

Each had a knife, haft outwards, in his hand; the head of each was sunk into his shoulders; each pair of eyes were fixed upon the other pair. Such a quarrel was no strange occurrence in that place; and the cause was the same as always —women.

Suddenly one of them sprang, bringing his knife hand round and up like a flash. There was a shriek from one of the women as the blade flashed in the light, but a man slammed his heavy hand over her lips and the accompanying oath reached even to where Blake and Tinker sat.

The knife did no more damage than to slit the shirt sleeve of the other fellow. He had not moved his feet in retreat, but had swayed his body with a rough, swift grace that saved him. And, on the forward recover of balance, he too struck.

He used a straight outward lunge that pressed close after the other's body as he sprang away. But his leap did not carry him far enough and he staggered as the blade plunged in between his ribs.

His opponent jerked the blade out and raised his arm to strike again. It seemed that his reeling vis-a-vis must go down after that one, terrible stab, but he kept his feet somehow and then, with a yell, rushed in blindly.

Both blades flashed and danced beneath the light. Thrust, thrust, cut, jab, stab! So quick were their movements that it was difficult for the naked eye to follow. There seemed to be a dozen knives flashing in a maze of circles; each fighter seemed endowed with half a dozen hands.

Time and again came the clash of steel upon steel as a blow was countered. But, again, came a soft thud that told of a thrust getting home. And, suddenly, it was all over.

The one who had been stabbed first suddenly threw up his left arm; the knife dropped to the floor from his right. He swayed drunkenly for a moment or two before sinking slowly to his knees, where he swayed from side to side as he fought desperately to conquer the black wave that was threatening to engulf him. But it was no use. The life blood was pumping out of his heart and into his lungs not to be returned, and as the arteries met nothing in their suction he slumped forward on to his face, rolled over and, after one sharp convulsion, lay still.

The victor brandished his blood-stained knife and laughed in triumph. The mob against the wall rushed towards him, joining in his triumph. The enormous patron behind the bar began to get down bottles, for he knew there would be a rush for fresh drinks. The whole body-sweating mob swayed as one, eager to catch the hand of the victor as they would have been as eager to congratulate the other had he been victorious.

Blake saw that the beads of perspiration were standing out on the lad's forehead. He gave vent to a low grunt to attract Tinker's attention and shot him a warning glance.

When he looked down again the body of the dead man had vanished. A man was already mopping away at the floor while another was sprinkling chalk. Some couples were already beginning to dance once more as the accordion whined into a fresh air.

Something seemed to tell Blake that he was being watched. He could feel eyes bent upon him, the urge of a strong will to know if he were a danger. He dragged his gaze back from the revolting spectacle beneath him and, turning his head slowly, found the dark eyes of the woman in green gazing directly into his.

He knew the moment of test was come. A devil-may-care grin

parted his lips as he tossed off the remains of his drink and rose to his feet. He swaggered across to the corner where the window of the serving hatch was cut and, leaning on the ledge, matched the woman's gaze.

"My faith, madame, but you are not slow here in the Green Woman. Not even in Barcelona could one see better knife work than that."

"The men of the quartier are quick enough with the knife, mon brave," she responded in a throaty voice that had probably been rich and not unpleasant in her youth. "And they are ready enough to use them if occasion warrants."

Blake was still smiling impudently.

"We, of Catalonia, know something of the knife as well, madame," he responded coolly. "And we know other things as well."

"As what, for instance, mon brave?"

"To know something far better worth looking at than a stupid knife fight, madame."

"The bull fight?"

"No, no, madame; a beautiful woman, one on whom the colour green sits divinely."

The patronne eyed him steadily for a few moments, but Blake held his gaze steady. Not the vestige of mockery did she see in those bold eyes of his. Then, most suddenly and most amazingly, she bridled and simpered. It was evident to Blake that his summing-up of her character had not been at fault. He had taken a chance on his form of approach. It was pretty safe betting that many a long year had passed since the patron had paid her a compliment; and it was equally likely that none of her ordinary customers would have dared do so even had he been inclined.

But this bold Catalonian, with the swagger air and the cocked round hat, was different. The whole wide bosom of the woman behind the hatch heaved in a gigantic sigh and she spoke in sharp reproof. But her eyes belied her words. And, all the time, her hand was reaching for a bottle of special sirop.

"Here, mon brave," she said when she had finished her reproof. "drink a glass of this and wash down your impudence. But take care the patron does not see."

"Madame, dear madame, I drink to the loveliness I see in your eyes. Ah! madame, were it not for the patron."

He rolled his eyes languishingly and drew a smile from her. But she did not see his hand pass swiftly inside his jacket and come out again. She guessed nothing until her gaze fell once more to the shelf of the hatch and she saw, directly beneath, a small twist of paper.

"What is this, mon brave? You have not written me an impudent love billet in anticipation?"

"Read it, madame."

So low was the whisper that it scarcely reached her. Slowly she took the paper up and spread it out. Then, at sight of the word it contained, the blood drained from her face. Her eyes, very different, in expression, lifted to Blake's. All her native caution and suspicion were predominant now.

But she did not say what was in her mind. Over his shoulder she saw a garcon approaching, and hurried words tumbled from her lips.

"Wait—I will speak to you later. Go!"

Blake edged away from the hatch, laughing at her again, as the waiter eyed him impatiently. Then he swaggered back to his table, hitting Tinker a heavy slap on the back, as he yelled for more drinks and slumped into his chair.

The die was cast. Heaven alone knew what would be the outcome.

It was past ten o'clock when Blake and Tinker entered the Green Woman. It was about half-past eleven when the knife fight took place. And from that the time dragged on until nearly one, before Blake received a signal from the woman in green.

He had been cutting at a hunk of bread with his knife. Now he wiped the blade on the sleeve of his jacket, drew the back of his hand across his mouth, and rose. He motioned for Tinker to remain where he was.

As he approached the serving-hatch he saw that the panel between the shelf and the floor was a door. The woman had opened it a little and motioned for him to crawl under.

He did so, finding himself in a small room that was lined with bottles. Under the shelves, against three walls, were small wine casks.

The moment he was inside the woman closed the panel and slipped a bolt, then she lowered the hatch window and fastened that. It was evident that no more drinks would be served from this room that night.

She descended from the stool on which her bulk had been

overflowing. He saw now that she was very short, and that her whole body was built on the same generous proportions as her bust. Just the same he could see that she had undoubtedly been of an attractive, voluptuous mould when younger, and that now, like so many persons who thicken, she could not realise that the youthful lines were gone. She was, in other words, a bundle of vanity.

But her own personal weaknesses had been thrust aside in face of this compelling bit of paper which this rough Catalonian had handed her. She was, of course, but a minor link in one of the lesser chains with which Blake was fumbling. She represented just one more step on the path which he had begun to follow back in London when he hauled a drug-stricken girl out of a Soho den.

Each step, small though it might be, was so much gain, however, and Sexton Blake wasn't missing any chances. The question was here —would he be able to make the next step, or would he be suspect?

She led him to a door in the opposite corner of the serving-room and into a small sitting-room which was so cluttered with gimcrack bits of furniture of the French provincial type that one could scarcely move for fear of colliding with some piece.

She closed the door and motioned him to a seat. He sank gingerly on to the edge of a tarnished gilt chair and waited while she opened another door and peered out into a narrow corridor. Then she closed it and came back, sinking into a low chair that groaned under her weight.

She fixed her eyes on him scarchingly.

"Where did you get that piece of paper, mon brave?"

"In Barcelona, madame."

"Why do you, a Catalonian sailor, come to me with such a thing?"

Blake shrugged.

"My purpose is not to be told, madame. I pass along with a word to be whispered to one who matters."

"Then why not proceed direct?" She asked sharply.

Blake had expected that question to arise and was prepared for it.

"You should know, madame, that the secret of strength is oblivion. I travel on behalf of one who is powerful. I carry a message of the greatest importance to one among those of whose existence you are but dimly aware. It is not for you or for me to question. You can give me the guide to the next step. I ask no more. As I go along I shall learn from one and another how to proceed until I have gained my objective. Were the way not so guarded the structure would long since have fallen."

"And if I refuse? How do I know you are not a spy?"

"You may refuse. There is nothing to compel you. But if you do so you will find that the Green Woman ceases to be included as a distributing point."

She was silent. On the face of it this fellow should be genuine enough. He had presented her with a paper on which was written the password which had been given her. He had brought it from Barcelona, which was also in order. There was one other password which could be used, but that should come from another place.

One password for "up the line," one password for "down the line." That was the arrangement. It all seemed in order. But this was the first time one had come whom she had not already known. What message could he bear? For whom was it intended?

She knew no more about the organisation in which she was a minor unit than that many small packages readied her which she in turn passed on. Whence they came, whither they went she did not know. She wasn't supposed to know.

Yet it was profitable. Ah! The wine shop did a good business and showed a good profit. But the trifling duty of passing on those little packages was far, far more profitable. She didn't want to lose that. Yet this fellow threatened that it would be taken away from her unless she did his bidding.

She could send him along one more step if she dared take the risk. But what if he were a spy? She had heard vague whispers of others who had tried to penetrate into the secret of the vast organisation of which even she knew so little. She had heard how they had died.

If this fellow—

"When do you wish to go forward?" she asked at last.

"At once, madame."

"Not to-night. It would be impossible."

"Then to-morrow,"

"It might be arranged," she admitted cautiously. "You will stay here to-night and we shall see. But I admit nothing, mon brave; that is clearly understood."

"It is understood, madame."

"Then send away your companion and I will show you a room."

"But no, madame. My companion travels with me. He is most useful. He fills a special need."

She frowned doubtfully.

"I don't like two of you."

"You need not worry about him, madame. He is only a sea-rover. He comes from anywhere. I need one with me, and he serves because he has the supreme stupidity."

"Then get him in here and I will show you a room."

"Bien, madame. You do well to serve the powerful one to-night. It will not be forgotten."

They went into the serving-room where the woman opened the panel and hissed to attract Tinker's attention. The lad turned, saw her beckoning, and rose.

She scrutinised him carefully when he was inside and the panel was closed, but the lad grinned back at her cheekily, and when she shot a sudden question at him in the argot of the Catalonian coast he came back at her with such an appalling mixture of every known port argot that a sailor could pick up that she threw up her hands.

Blake was smiling in the impudent manner he had adopted.

"You see, madame, I told you," he remarked.

"Come," was all she said.

Chapter 5.   The Assassin.

THEY mounted two flights of narrow, precipitous stairs.

The room into which they were ushered was small, musty-smelling and contained only one small window that was protected with wooden bars. One who was not well acquainted with the quarter might wonder why bars were useful in a window so high; but Blake knew that the old houses were tumbled, hotch-potch up the hillside, so that the roof of one might be the door step of the other, as it were.

It would not be an easy room to escape from. That much was plain. And it would be equally a nasty hole to be besieged in. But Blake expected to find far more dangerous quarters than that before his quest was over.

Light was furnished by a single fly-specked bulb that dangled from a cord in the middle of the ceiling. There was a big feather bed, none too clean of sheets and blankets, a couple of rickety wooden chairs, a washstand and a collection of enamelled-ware toilet articles. A most, depressing retreat, if one were easily affected by one's surroundings.

Madame wasted no time in bidding them "bon-soir." When she had closed the door they stood listening while she creaked her way down the stairs. Then Blake examined the door.

He did not speak, but by signs Tinker gathered that there was no means of locking it on the inside. He watched while Blake made a tour of the room, searching for any place where it might be possible for a hidden watcher to spy upon them. But the walls seemed solid enough.

Suddenly he switched out the light and, reaching for the lad's arm, guided him along to the barred window. They could just see out, and now though the rain had stopped the wind was still sweeping round the building in strong gusts.

A moon hung in the sky with clouds scudding across its face. Beneath it they could see the lights in the harbour and the revolving lantern of a lighthouse farther out.

The sight seemed but to accentuate their isolation, for each knew what lay between them and the safety they represented.

Blake drew back and put his lips close to the lad's ear.

"Listen well," Tinker heard him breathe. "I don't trust that dame a little bit. I'm puzzled that the man didn't take any part in the talk.

He must be in the thing as much as she is. She is wary and I think, suspicious. If anything should break we would find ourselves in a nasty position. We don't know what moment a word of warning might come through from Barcelona. So we won't undress —yet. Give me a hand with the bed. We'll 'cook' it so it will look as if we are under the clothes. The moonlight will show it up quite plainly."

They moved cautiously, one to each side of the big bed, and worked away with blankets and pillows and bolsters until they had formed two long bulges that looked as if two persons lay there.

Then Blake drew the lad to the corner nearest the door. It would act as a screen in case anyone entered. More precautions they could not take.

They squatted on the floor, and once more Blake whispered to the lad.

"Lean up against the wall, and get some sleep if you can, Tinker. I'll keep watch for a period, and you can take a turn later."

Tinker would have been ready enough to take first turn, but he knew how useless it would be to argue with Blake. He was a seasoned campaigner, and proved it by wedging himself in the corner angle of the two walls and drowsing off within a few minutes.

As for Blake, he had never been more awake and on the qui vive in his life. He knew that the danger of a warning following them from Barcelona was a very real one.

He had gained his point there through a combination of daring bluff, heavy bribery, and no little cunning. But he knew that the risk of betrayal was great.

It had been the same in each other place he had stopped. He had evaded the consequences so far, but that did not mean he would be able to go on in such luck.

All he could do was to keep his guard every moment, not to allow himself to be "jumped," sleeping or waking, and then to deal with the danger as it came.

Himself, he had no desire for sleep. His mind was too active, planning the next step if, on the morrow, he should get out of the woman in green the morsel of information he was after.

He was puzzled, too, as he had told Tinker, that the patron had not joined his wife in the discussion. He knew it was pretty good betting that he knew long before this why he had come. What would he do? Would he approve the course his wife had taken? Or would he be even more wary? The night might show.

Just how long he had been squatting on the floor before a sound close at hand caught his attention, Blake could not have said. All the time he had been conscious of the general, normal sounds of the house and quarter —of snatches of maudlin song, of sudden bursts of cursing and shouting, of a door being slammed, of the high-pitched voices of women, of hysterical laughter, of sobs, of screams, of the faint tinkle of glasses and, from the distant harbour, the deep bass of a ship's siren —a homely, comforting break in the sinister song of the quarter.

Gradually they had died away. Not that the quarter was sinking into slumber. On the contrary. Now, in the darkest hours of the nights did the rats venture farther afield on their prowling. But the Green Woman had become quiet; its business would start again when the rats returned.

The first thing that caught Blake's attention was what he knew to be a creaking stair. He had marked them well on the way up. It was a habit of his not only to take that particular notice of a staircase, of any flight, but to count the steps as well. Those two simple precautions had saved his life on more than one occasion.

He could guess fairly accurately that someone was mounting the first flight. Nothing extraordinary in that. The patron and patronne might sleep on the first floor; the garcons might sleep on that floor, or on the one where he and Tinker had been given a room; though, for the latter, Blake had only noticed one other door on this level.

He leaned forward a little, straining to catch the next sound. It came after an interval, a double creak and, so quickly did the one follow the other, that he felt pretty sure neither the fat proprietor nor his corpulent wife could have negotiated them so rapidly.

Was it a garcon? He shifted his position until he was on his knees. Then he laid a cautious hand on Tinker's shoulder. The lad was awake instantly.

Blake got to his feet, drawing the lad after him. They stood close to the wall, their heads thrust forward listening intently. No other creak came to them but, a few moments later, they heard something moving outside the door.

Blake gave Tinker's arm a warning pressure and flattened himself still more against the wall. Then he grew rigid as a metallic rattle came to their ears —faint, but enough to tell them that someone was cautiously opening the chamber door.

They heard nothing more for the moment, but something indefinable, some subtle change in the atmosphere of the room, warned them that the door had swung open. Which meant that the intruder must be on the very threshold.

Who was this who came with such sinister caution in the night. What was his purpose?

Still they waited. The moonlight was streaming in through the window, making a distinct, barred pattern, that lay partly on the bed, partly on the floor.

Out of the corner of his eye Blake could see the dim outline of the heaps he and Tinker had made. From that distance they looked more than ever like sleeping humans beneath the blankets.

Then he was as tense as a cat, for someone had stepped fully into the room. They saw the blur of a figure that must have been moving in stockinged feet, so noiselessly did he tread. It wasn't the patron. The bulk was not sufficient.

It was a big man, even allowing for the fact that his bulk might appear exaggerated in the quarter light due to the moon. But, for all his bulk, he moved as stealthily and as certainly as a tiger on the stalk for, almost before they were aware of it, he was in the middle of the room.

He seemed to turn his head a little and stare directly towards where they stood in the shadow. Blake was ready to rush forward the moment he gave the slightest sign that he knew they were there. Indeed, as he distinctly saw the hollows of the man's eyes, shadowed, looking empty as if set in a naked skull, he almost launched himself forward.

But the other turned his head back, and began creeping once more towards the bed.

Then they saw his arm go up, silhouetted distinctly against the moonlight; and they saw something else —they caught the gleam of the fitful beam on naked steel as it paused aloft.

His purpose was plain enough now.

Blake knew that he had no need to add any warning touch to the orders he had given to Tinker. The lad was standing so close to him that he could feel every rise and fall of his lungs, could actually follow every beat of his heart. He was, he could guess, waiting on whatever move he made, though he could follow plainly what was going forward.

Then the intruder was close to the bed. He bulked against the moonlight that had been lying on the coverlet, breaking its continuity. His head was plainly silhouetted for a brief moment as he leant forward, a round bullet head that might or might not have had a skull-fitting cap on it.

They saw the knife raised aloft still higher. They saw the brief pause before the downward stroke. Then the man struck, driving it with terrific force into the nearest lump of bedclothes.

And then Sexton Blake launched himself forward, for he knew that the first moment of contact would tell the assassin the truth.

He was right. Before he had covered half the distance the would-be murderer had given vent to a low, startled oath. He was tugging at the knife when he heard Blake coming. He flung himself backwards and aside, and straightened up just in time to meet Blake's rush.

Then they crashed.

Blake had no intention of employing any finesse or orthodox means of attack. He was determined, by any means in his power, to scotch this assassin of the darkness as quickly as possible. And that determination was expressed in a terrific punch to the solar plexus as he lunged in.

The assassin slammed back against the wall with a grunt as the outraged diaphragm heaved upwards. But he kept his feet, and only a swift side-step saved Blake from the knife that was jabbed down savagely.

It was only then he realised the other had succeeded in dragging it out of the blankets before straightening up. He drove in two swift punches with his right then he shot up his left to try and grasp the other's wrist.

They stood thus braced to body, the one holding his arm high, the other striving to drag it down.

Blake felt the wooden bars of the window against his knuckles. The touch gave him an idea. With a quick yielding he allowed his antagonist's hand to go back, then he jammed against it with all his strength.

Hand and knife were forced between two of the bars where the blade was caught. The other realised too late how his weapon had been trapped. He retaliated by sinking his teeth into the flesh of Blake's neck, tearing at it as ferociously as any cornered rat.

The pain was excruciating. It drove Blake to a fury that lent a vicious sting to the short rights that he kept sending in to the other's body.

It seemed as if he might as well have hammered the wall for all the effect they appeared to have. But he knew what was behind them and he knew they must get through to something vital if he could continue them.

The collapse came even before he expected it. One moment the other was ranging on like grim death with his teeth, the next his head dropped away and he gave a deep groan of agony as his heart flinched under the blows.

The knife clattered to the window sill from the nerveless fingers. Blake could hear it strike a roof a little distance below and then came a faint clattering sound as it tumbled down the tiles to another resting place.

He could see Tinker, hovering close, ready to take a hand. But the lad knew from long experience that he was not to interfere unless absolutely necessary. Besides, his job was to watch the door to see that no fresh assailants came.

Nor did Blake need him now. A dull anger was making him as savage as the man he faced. Breaking away, he sent in a hail of blows that drove the other along the wall, ducking, trying to get far enough away to use his feet.

But Blake gave him no chance. He knew what one of those rats could do with his feet once he got an opening. He followed him, bringing in uppercut after uppercut to send his head up, then following with a pile-driver from the shoulder that would drive the other's head against the wall with a force that threatened to crack the skull.

It was amazing what punishment he took without going down. Time and again Blake thought he had him, and time and again he slid out from under.

It was only when Blake saw the open door close at hand that he realised they had fought right around the room. He had no time to wonder if the noise had attracted the attention of those below. He was leaving all that to Tinker.

It must have been the sight of the open door that brought realisation of failure to the assassin, for, when they readied that spot, he bent double, as if Blake's last blow had done its work. So well did he simulate acute distress that Blake actually held his arm; and that brief moment was the other's advantage.

With amazing speed he straightened up and made to dash through the door. Tinker gasped a quick warning. Blake leaped forward, and the pair crashed just outside the door.

The assassin swung with an appalling curse and, in a fresh access of fury, drove into Blake like a maniac. Blake gave way a step, taking the punishment on his arms and head, watching his groin in case a foot came lunging up.

Then, suddenly, he feinted, drew back, measured his distance as well as the gloom would permit, and let out his right with all the force of shoulder and body behind it.

Crack!

It was like the snapping of a bone. Then:

Crash!

A splintering of wood followed as the assassin went back against the flimsy wooden banisters that were the only thing between him and the staircase well. Then there followed a heavy thud as he hit the steps about half way down and a series of lesser bumps as he tumbled to the bottom.

Blake paused on the sheer edge of the well and peered down. He could see nothing, hear nothing. Tinker was crouching beside him, and whispered that he would go down. But Blake restrained him.

"Leave him alone," he whispered back. "If he is dead it won't do any good. If he lives, he will be attended to. Come back into the room."

They returned to the chamber and closed the door. There was no attempt at concealment in Blake's movements now, for he switched on the light and surveyed the wreckage of one chair and a table. Then he made for the wash-stand and motioned for the lad to bathe his mangled throat.

Not until the lad had done what was possible did Blake make further comment. He spoke as he walked towards the bed.

"We'll turn in actually, now," he said in ordinary tones, speaking in Catalonian. "I am sure the patron cannot be aware that there are undesirable characters in his house. But I do not think any more will worry us to-night."

And they did take off their outer clothes, though, despite the words he had used for the effect of any surreptitious listener, Blake and the lad took two-hour watches until dawn came.

NOTHING disturbed them until a slatternly girl appeared with a can of warmish water.

She made no conversation; nor did she offer to bring them anything to eat.

Blake and Tinker, the former smoking a caporal cigarette, sat on the side of the bed until she was gone. Then they washed, taking turns at the rather grubby bit of towel that had been left.

So far, neither had looked down the stairs to see what daylight might reveal. Blake had been a little curious to know if the girl would mention the smashed banisters, but since she kept silence he was not inclined to opened the subject.

On emerging from the room to descend to the café, on the ground floor, they were able to see exactly the extent of the damage to the banisters. A good half dozen of the wooden rods had been knocked clean out, three or four were broken off at varying lengths, and the top rail was smashed through, hanging by a splintered break at one end. It was proof of the power Blake had put behind that last terrific punch.

They ignored it, descending the stairs to the next floor. There was no sign of the assassin. They hadn't expected to find any at this hour. But there were some dark patches on the floor that could have been made by blood.

On reaching the café they found the patronne on duty behind the zinc bar. She bade them a "bon jour," to which they responded briefly. Then she asked if they would have coffee and rolls —a suggestion to which Blake returned an affirmative.

"Go to the upper floor, mon brave," she returned. "The garcon will serve you there."

Blake led the way to the stairs that took them to the same place where he and the lad had sat the previous night. He was thinking hard as he ascended. He was puzzled, deeply so.

There hadn't been the slightest flicker in the woman's eye to tell him what might be in her mind about the events of the night. He didn't know whether the absence of the patron meant anything or not. He realised it might be that he was not accustomed to come on duty until a later hour.

There was something sinister, however, in the fact that murder could be attempted in the place and the whole affair treated as if it had not occurred.

Yet there was no denying those smashed banisters; there was no getting away from the fact that the would-be assassin must have been found lying at the foot of the stairs.

Was he dead? If so, what had become of the body? Or had he only been unconscious? As a matter of fact, his body was even then floating in the outer basin, to be picked up later that same day.

But the chief question that worried Blake was motive. Who was the fellow, he kept asking himself again and again. Had he followed them from Barcelona? If so, then he must have warned the patron and patronne of the Green Woman that there was something fishy about the Catalonian sailor and his youthful companion.

If that were so what would she do?

As a matter of fact that is exactly how the case stood, though Blake was never to know the exact truth. Later on, events were to enable him to conclude that his deductions were correct. But, at the moment, he was all at sea.

Even while he had been in the private room with the patronne the night before, a man had entered the lone shop and had passed a private code-word to the patron behind his zinc bar.

No sooner did the woman return downstairs from showing Blake and Tinker to their room than she knew what the man had to say.

He had come from Barcelona. As Blake feared he had been betrayed by the one here who had taken his bribe. Nothing definite beyond that was told to the couple at the Green Woman for the simple reason that the messenger who had been detailed to follow the pair to Marseilles knew nothing definite about their identity.

Suspicion was enough, however, for a decision to be made that this mysterious Catalonian and his companion should be killed before they had a chance to do any real mischief. The bodies could be disposed of easily enough. There was the inner basin, the outer basin, the great harbour, the whole vast Mediterranean.

It was never anticipated that the tables would be turned as Blake had turned them. And the truth of the matter was that the woman was in a state of no little uneasiness as to what steps the Catalonian would take next. She and her husband had decided to say nothing unless the Catalonian should mention the matter. Then they would know what line to take.

She was all the more mystified, then, that he behaved as if

nothing at all had occurred. Yet she knew that this man who moved up the stairs had missed death by inches in the dark hours of the night. She knew that he had so well defended himself that he had hurled his would-be assassin through the staircase banisters to the bottom where he had been found with a broken neck. She knew those ugly purple marks on the side of his neck had not been there when she talked with him the evening before. Therefore, they must have been received during the struggle.

Yet he said nothing. He looked as calm and self-contained as ever. Why? She asked herself the question as frequently as Blake asked himself the other. And the more she did so the more uneasy she became. A strange fear began to tug at her heart. Who was this man? Had it been a terrible mistake to attempt his assassination? Might he possibly be one of the powers in the organisation? Might she and her man suffer unimaginable tortures as punishment?

She could only arrive at one decision. The thing was beyond her capacity. She could not deal with it. Others of more knowledge and greater wit must discover the truth. She would send him on the next step. Then she would wash her hands of the whole matter unless he should mention the events of the night. In that case she would have to trust to her quickness of wit.

But the Catalonians did not speak of it. He and his youth companion drank their coffee and ate their rolls slowly, enjoyably. Then he lit a caporal and, seeing the woman behind the hatch window, rose and strolled across.

"I come to pay for my room, madame." he said easily. "For the food for myself and young friend I will pay the garcon."

She shrugged her fat shoulders. Their eyes held together.

"It is nothing, mon brave. You will accept the hospitality of the house, I hope."

"As you will, madame. We depart in a few minutes. You have something to give me?"

Her eyes flickered under his steady stare; but she managed a smile.

Only the garcon and Tinker were anywhere near, and they were well out of earshot. She leaned close to the shelf, her bust billowing over the edge until the green dress touched Blake's arm.

"You know the Silver Tower cafe in the city, mon brave?"

"But, yes. I have been in Marseilles before."

"If you go there and seek one known as Gros Jean you will learn something you wish to know. Find Gros Jean and give to him the same word you brought to me. That will be sufficient."

"I may say that I come from the Green Woman?"

She hesitated; then:

"As you will."

"Merci, madame. And now, au revoir or, shall it be, good-bye?"

"We hope to see you again, mon brave."

Blake smiled, and taking her hand bent as if to kiss it. But instead he fixed her hard with his eyes in which she saw something she knew not for mockery or threat.

"You and the patron, madame, you enjoy good health, I trust," he said softly.

"But —but, yes, mon brave, the very best."

"Then let us hope it will continue so," he returned in the same tone. "It would be a pity, madame, if something happened to cut short your life or that of the patronne. Life is uncertain, as some of us have discovered. I think, madame, that, after all it will be only au revoir."

With that he touched his lips to the back of her podgy hand, smiled into her eyes once more and turned away, leaving behind him as frightened a specimen of fat womanhood as had ever trembled in that unsavoury quarter.

Blake swaggered across to where Tinker still sat. He tossed some coins on the table for the garcon and spoke a curt word to the lad. Tinker rose at once, and together the pair made for the stairs. Just before he went down Blake turned once more and sent a swift look back towards the woman in green. Then, as he followed Tinker, the level of the floor hid her from view.

It was raining again, not heavily, but a soft drizzle was misting in from the bay. They did not talk as they descended the hill towards the street that paralleled the basin.

Both of them knew perfectly well that many pairs of eyes were following their course; and it was safe betting that, if the assassin had been killed by his fall, they were a marked pair.

It was not until they were getting well along into the actual turmoil of the docks that Tinker ventured a question.

"What is the next move, guv'nor? Any luck with old twenty stone?"

"I'm not sure yet, young 'un. We are going to the Silver Tower to find a man known as Gros Jean."

"That means Big Jack."

"Quite so. After that, we shall see."

"Did she say anything about last night?"

"Not a word."

"That's one of the queerest things I've ever struck, guv'nor. They must have known that bird was going to try and bump us off; yet you'd think it never happened."

"I agree with you, Tinker. It is certainly odd. They knew about it all right. We don't know what has become of the would-be assassin, but the smashed banisters are there still as mute evidence. Nor do we know what has become of the patron. But I'll say the woman had her nerve with her all right."

"Do you think she bluffed you in giving you that name?"

"I don't think so —somehow. She may be suspicious, but she isn't quite sure. And she wouldn't possess either enough knowledge or authority to do more than was done last night."

"Do you think they inspired that attack on us?"

"No. I believe we were followed from Barcelona, young 'un. You will recall that I told you I had not much trust for our informant there. It took too much to bribe him. Had he taken less I should have had more faith in him. But it looks as if he had at least given us the correct password. It strikes me, young 'un, that we are on the right trail so far, and that there is a certain amount of suspicion against us. But each is leaving it to someone else to take steps to remove us as a danger. Last night was the first definite attempt."

"If that was a sample we'll see plenty more," grunted the lad.

"It was, I should say, only a mild beginning," agreed Blake.

They took the ferry across the basin which brought them to the business section of the city. There they continued on foot until they came to the Cannebiere, that famous thoroughfare which is the centre of the shopping district. From here Blake proceeded on past the Bourse, and then, by, means of many narrow, confusing streets, arrived at the old basin. And here, on the corner of a street that had been in use since the days when the Roman Empire ruled the world, he turned into the notorious Tour d'Argent, or Silver Tower.

Chapter 7.   The Silver Tower.

THERE may be some doubt as to how this particular place got its name, but there can be none about the class of business for which it caters. It is the haunt of seafaring folk of every nation, and, on any day or evening, one can find a seat cheek by jowl with a Levantine out of Alexandria or a coast mongrel from South America as easily as with a Bluenose from Eastern Canada or a hardbitten gin-slinger from up Shanghai way.

Blake and Tinker knew the cafe well. It had a good enough name as such places go. There was never any talk of 'shang-hai-ing' a man there; the drinks were what they purported to be; the food was better than indifferent. It was just a fair-to-middling place where sailor men foregather, and it was popular because it was always brightly lighted, had some music and sported some girls who were ready to make friends. The average roamer doesn't ask for much more.

But what Blake didn't know was whether the man called Gros Jean was a member of the staff of the cafe or a client. That was something he would have to learn after entering. Nor did he know, what sort of person to look for, although, as Tinker had said, the name meant 'Big Jack' so it seemed reasonable to be on the look-out for a beefy specimen.

There were not many people in the place at that hour of the morning. A few sat here and there drinking coffee and rum; fewer still were recovering from what was obviously a 'hang-over' from the night before.

Somewhere about eleven o'clock the place would begin to crowd up, and from that on until two or three business would be brisk enough.

The condition of things suited Blake. It meant that they could choose a table in a spot where they could have a good view or most of the cafe; and they would be able to make a more leisurely study of those who were already there and those who came along, than if the place were crowded.

Although they had already had coffee and rolls, Blake ordered the same thing again. The table they had chosen was in one corner under a balcony, rather gloomy now that the artificial lights were not turned on. Its shadow suited them, however, for unless one took the trouble to approach close one could not distinguish them very clearly.

41

Blake's first care was to make a study of the three men, the patron, he guessed, and two youths who were behind the long zinc bar —a much longer bar than that at the Green Woman, for it was a much larger place.

None of those seemed to answer to the description of Gros Jean as he had fixed it in his mind, so he transferred his attention to the waiters.

He knew, of course, that the morning shift, now on duty, would by no means comprise the full list. But he soon came to the conclusion that if Gros Jean were a big person and a waiter he was certainly not in the cafe at that moment; for none of the white-aproned men who were moving about filled the bill.

Tinker, in the meantime, had been making a study of the various customers. Many of those were beefy persons, but where size might have fitted what he sought, dress ruled the subject out, for each was obviously a seafaring man.

Their eyes met at last, and each gave a negative shake of the head. Then, jointly, they began to make a quick survey of each customer as he entered.

A good score or more had come in when Blake touched Tinker's foot under the table. The lad made an almost imperceptible response with his head. He had spotted the person Blake was indicating, in the same moment.

Nor was it easy to ignore the newcomer. He was an enormous man, fully nineteen stone in weight and well over six foot in height. His limbs, head and feet were built on the same generous scale as his body, and had there been any doubt that he was the "Gros Jean" for whom they were on the look-out, it was settled a moment later, when he pushed his ponderous way past a table where two men were sitting.

Both of them gave him greeting, and, where they sat, Blake, and the lad could hear one of them say distinctly:

"Ah! Gros Jean, mon vieux. How do you find yourself? Sit down, mon ami, and take something."

The big man grunted something which the listeners could not distinguish. He seemed to speak thickly through a small mouth that was only a button set in great rolls of chin.

It seemed, though, that he did not wish to delay, for he pushed on, and the watchers saw him approach a table in a corner under the balcony which was about as secluded as their own.

A solitary individual sat here, a dark-skinned man that might have been a Levantine. Seeing that Gros Jean was about to sit down, a waiter hurried with an iron-framed chair on which he balanced his great bulk. Then he turned his head slowly, and, although they did not meet his gaze, Blake and Tinker had a feeling that not a single thing or person in the cafe missed those sharp little piggy eyes.

Then he turned back and began to carry on a low-toned conversation with his vis-a-vis. The thought came to Blake that the other man might easily be a messenger from the Green Woman on the look-out for Gros Jean to give him warning about the Catalonian. And, before very much time had passed, he was to discover that this surmise was only too correct.

Now that he felt sure this big individual could only be the one he was seeking, he cudgelled his brains to think up a means of approach. Unless some lucky accident threw them together, it seemed that he would have to intercept the other boldly and ask for a word in private.

And, in fact, this was what he finally decided to do.

Gros Jean had been sitting at the other table for a quarter of an hour or so when he got to his feet. He stood hesitant, as if trying to make up his mind whether to leave the place or not.

It was then that Blake, with a quick warning glance at Tinker, got to his feet and swaggered across to where the big one stood. If Gros Jean saw him coming, he gave no sign until Blake was almost touching his elbow.

But then he turned with such swiftness as to startle Blake. Had the latter not had all his years of training behind him, he might have been caught off his guard by that manoeuvre.

As it was he showed no outward sign that he was taken by surprise. He met the piggy eyes with the same impudent grin he had adopted at the Green Woman, and before he had time to speak Gros Jean spoke.

"Why do you approach me like this, cochon? What do you want?"

"Pardon, monsieur, but I seek Monsieur Gros Jean. I understand that you are he."

"Bien. And if so?"

"I crave a word in private, monsieur."

"From whom do you come with a message?"

"It is not possible to answer that question here, monsieur. I will explain in private. I shall satisfy monsieur of my credentials."

"I like you not, fellow, but —come."

He started to turn away, leaving it for Blake to follow. Blake made a swift gesture to Tinker which caused the lad to get to his feet and hurry towards him.

Thus in single file they went through the main cafe to an inner room. Here Gros Jean spoke a few words to a waiter which Blake could not hear.

The waiter unlocked a door on the right and opened it. Gros Jean passed through and Blake and Tinker followed to find themselves in a long corridor off which several rooms appeared to open, if one were to judge by the number of closed doors.

It was plain enough by now that if Gros Jean had no financial interest in the Silver Tower he was a very privileged person. Blake thought he was hitting the truth pretty close when he surmised that Gros Jean was a very important factor in the secret trade of drugs in the port of Marseilles —a hint that would have been deeply appreciated by the chief of police of the city.

Gros Jean passed the first door on the left and turned to that on the right. From his pocket he took a bunch of keys with which he unlocked it, again proving his privilege.

He walked in, leaving it for the other two to follow. But as soon as they were inside the door he turned the lock. Then he moved across to a flat-topped desk and sat in a chair of such size that it must have been provided specially for him.

"Stand there," he ordered, pointing to the front of the desk.

Blake obeyed. Tinker took up a place beside his master. Thus the two stood waiting.

"What are you?" asked Gros Jean sharply.

"Catalonian, monsieur," was Blake's prompt response.

"And why do you seek me? Come now, cochon, no lies."

"I travel on a certain road, monsieur. I bear a message for one who sits in great power. My instructions are that, though the road be long, each step will be indicated. Thus far have I come. I crave the goodness of monsieur to indicate the next step."

"A good story, you son of a dog. But that doesn't account for the dead man at the Green Woman."

The fat was in the fire, and Blake knew it. Those words were sufficient proof that warning had reached him. It was a bad check. It seemed as if all those weeks of patient work and danger had gone for nothing.

Would bluff serve him now? It didn't seem likely. There was knowledge in those shrewd little eyes.

"Well, what have you to say? Give me the word you bring, and I will see."

It couldn't make matters worse by complying with the demand. If he knew all about what had happened at the Green Woman, then he would know that he— Blake —was in possession of the key word. So he leaned forward a little and spoke it.

"Twenty-eight."

The actual voicing of the word seemed to act upon Gross Jean like a shot of dope. Some indistinguishable sound came from his lips as he came out of his chair, and, with an agility amazing in one of his bulk, rushed round the desk, arms outstretched and threats tumbling breathlessly from his button of a mouth.

"Ah! Cochon! Pig and son of pigs! Villain! Apache! Assassin! Liar! I will take you in my hands and break you in pieces. I will pick you limb from limb as I would pick a chicken. I will show you how Gros Jean breaks a man and makes of him a pulp. This I do —thus."

Gros Jean may have broken many a man with those huge hands and great arms of his. Once within his grasp one as physically powerful even as Blake would be helpless. The man had the strength of a grizzly, and the ruthlessness of a tiger. As dangerous a man as Blake had ever faced.

And Gros Jean looked for an easy smashing of this fellow who had dared to probe into the secret circle of which he was a unit. Those others, the people at the Green Woman, the fool in Barcelona who had sent this cochon to Marseilles, others whom he might have fooled were small fry compared to him, Gros Jean.

He was one of importance in the organisation. He knew the actual identity of the powerful one who sat in the centre of the web. He, Gros Jean, was one of the directors for France. And this, the first time anyone had got thus far, must be marked by a swift punishment.

He would kill him and the youth with his naked hands. He would have them thrown into the sea. That would settle that.

And it certainly looked as if he would succeed, for his arms were already about Blake before the latter was able to elude his rush. Then the great muscles tautened, and Tinker stood appalled at the ease with which he pressed Blake to him, held him off the floor as if he had been a child, closed his arm still more until the look of agony that flashed into Blake's eyes spurred the lad into action.

He knew he might as well tackle the side of a building as to pit his strength against Gros Jean. Yet he must do something, and that quickly.

His eyes darted about desperately. He saw, on the desk, a curiously fashioned paper weight. It looked like black stone or marble and, snatching it up, he felt it heavy in his hand.

He flung round in time to hear an involuntary groan wrung from the lips of the utterly helpless Blake. He saw Blake's eyes beginning to start from his head —expected each moment to hear his ribs smash under that awful pressure.

Then, with all his strength, he struck at the back of Gros Jean's head.

There was a crackling sound as if a giant egg had split. There was a staggering of the giant form as the arms, suddenly inert, fell away from Blake who slid to his knees, half-paralysed.

Tinker stood ready to strike again while he watched the giant totter back and forth while a whistling noise came from his little mouth. Then he collapsed, it seemed, in every joint of his body, sinking like a pricked balloon to the floor where he rolled over and lay still.

It was a full two minutes before Blake could force himself to his feet. He said nothing to the lad. It wasn't necessary; but he knew that in that one terrific blow Tinker had saved his life.

He got slowly to his knees and passed his hand along the back of Gros Jean's skull. When he took his fingers away he sent a glance at Tinker.

"It will be a considerable time before this bird chirps again, young 'un —thanks to you. You have cracked his skull for a good three inches, and I fancy it will need to be trepanned before he will know what happened to him. Watch that door, young 'un. I'm going to go through his pockets. Then we'll get out of here."

He worked fast, taking a remarkably small collection of articles from Gros Jean's pockets. Some of them he thrust back again, but a few he transferred to his own keeping, among them being a well-stuffed leather wallet which was destined to play an important part in the dangerous game which he and Tinker were following. Then he rose, and after listening at the door signed to the lad.

"Come on," he whispered, "let's beat it."

EVEN had Gros Jean been able to give a detailed description of the two fugitives it would have needed no little skill to lay hands on Blake and Tinker once they got away from the Tower of Silver.

That description, Gros Jean was unable to provide. Nor would he be of any use in that way for many weeks to come. Blake had made no mistake in appraising the effect of the blow Tinker had struck.

As for anyone else in the cafe, the only person who was able to give anything like a description of the pair was the dark-skinned man with whom Gros Jean had been speaking; and he was only certain about the general outward appearance.

Although it was he who had brought Gros Jean the warning from the Green Woman, he had not known that the two at the other table were those about whom he spoke.

Nearly quarter of an hour passed after Blake and Tinker slipped into the street before Gros Jean was found. It was nothing strange for him to make use of that private room for which he paid an annual fee; and it was also quite an ordinary thing for him to take all sorts and conditions or people into it for private confab.

But when a garcon did find him the alarm was spread at once, and it was only natural that it should be concluded that the two rough-looking Catalonians should be suspect. When it appeared obvious that Gros Jean's wallet was gone that suspicion was quite definite.

Blake counted on this. He knew perfectly well that a hue and cry would be started which would comb the city from one end to the other. But he figured against this that their pursuers would not go to the police. It would be a case in which every crook in Marseilles would be acting as a detective, judge and executioner in one, and heaven help the fugitives if any of that mob got their hands on them.

The first thing to do was to alter their appearance radically so as to gain a few hours at least. Then to put Marseilles behind them as rapidly as possible.

The first was not difficult. Knowing the place as well as he did Blake had in his mind two or three dens where he could effect a change of disguise and no questions asked. He knew that the search would concentrate more intensely about the waterfront than to the landward side. They had come by sea, and it would be natural to conclude that, being sailors, they would attempt to get away by sea.

48

To counter this Blake decided that they should disguise themselves as peasants. And as soon as they had left the Tour d'Argent well behind, had passed through the throngs on the Cannebiere, and were in an entirely different part of the city, he led the way at once to the shop of a Levantine with whom he had done business before; though that individual never dreamed on any occasion that he was outfitting an English detective.

In the privacy of a back room with the various items Blake purchased about them, he set to work to fix up, first Tinker, then himself.

He worked fast but thoroughly, for he knew they might have to pass close inspection the moment they stepped into the street. The two jobs took a precious three-quarters of an hour, but when he had finished they bore only one resemblance to the pair who had entered by the front door— that was in the difference in height. But to counteract that Blake adopted a slight limp as soon as they stepped into the alley at the back, and, in this fashion, they made for the central railway station.

No one challenged them on the way nor in the station. There was a local train leaving for Arles in about half an hour, so, after buying two third-class tickets, they took themselves to a quiet corner of the big waiting-room.

They climbed into their carriage only about two minutes before the train pulled out. Right up to the last minute Blake was on the qui vive, and at one moment when a rough-looking fellow paused to look deliberately into their compartment, his arm stiffened for action. But the other passed on, seeking, apparently, someone else.

Descending at Arles they had a wait of only some twelve minutes before the express for Toulon and the Riviera thundered in from Paris.

Once more they sought the obscurity of a third-class carriage, and there they remained huddled in their deep collars until the train pulled into Toulon.

They got out once more, and, once through the barrier, Blake led the way swiftly through a maze of narrow streets which he knew well. He was making for a certain cheap pension, a place of repute none too good, but suitable for their purpose.

It lay in the lower part of the town on the side of the harbour opposite the great naval yards. And while the quarter was rough enough, it was by no means of the type of the thieves' quarter in

Marseilles, for in Toulon the supervision of residents is thorough. France does not permit doubtful persons to reside too close to her big arsenals and dockyards.

Using the name of a certain dive-keeper in Paris, Blake succeeded in gaining entrance to the house. It was a tall, narrow house, dingy and even more musty than the Green Woman. But it meant temporary safety, and if things went as Blake hoped, they would be able to hit the trail again before many hours were passed. The chief thing just then was to vanish from the face of the earth so far as the friends of Gros Jean were concerned, and had he been in Marseilles he would have seen how well they had managed to do so, for that city was still being combed in search of them.

They sallied forth to get some food, but when that duty was attended to they returned to their room on the top floor of the lodging-house, and there, behind a locked door, Blake set to work to make a detailed examination of what he had taken from Gros Jean's pockets.

Most of the junk could be discarded after a brief glance. It was the wallet that interested him most. It contained in money some two thousand francs, which Blake appropriated for the time being. There were half a dozen letters couched in such terms as to make one think they referred only to passing incidents of interest only to the writer and the recipient, but which Blake concluded shrewdly held a hidden meaning.

Some cards with addresses he also gave but a superficial attention; the folder of a club in Marseilles he kept for further reference. And then he came upon a sheet of folded paper, very thin, and bearing some peculiar characters that caught his close attention, for among them he noticed the same number as that which had been given him as a key-word in Marseilles, and which he had found only too efficacious.

Firstly, in the upper left-hand corner of the paper was written:
"SOKTIM"
and, beneath that, two numbers, as follows:
28   38
There was absolutely nothing else on the paper.

Did that number, thirty-eight, have any connection with the same number given to him, Blake asked himself. If so, what could be its meaning, and what could be its connection with the other number, twenty-eight?

Further, what might be the relation of each or both to the letters above?

He studied them again. S O K T I M. Separated, they told him nothing, SOKTIM. Placed close together as if to form a word they were no more enlightening.

Yet he had a feeling that they must have some connection with the numbers, and the latter with his mission. But what? What? What?

He pushed the paper across to Tinker, and lighting a caporal, got to his feet. At this moment he would have given a good deal for his favourite briar, but he knew that such a pipe would soon attract attention, and he would rather smoke the strong caporals than tackle one of the cheap country bruyeres. So insistent was he that whatever their disguise it should contain no flaws, he would not even carry an English pipe hidden. There was no telling when they might be searched.

Pulling away at the cigarette he began to pace up and down, visualising the two numbers in his mind, trying to fit them this way and that with the letters, trying to connect them in some way with the events which had taken place since he left London.

Now and then he paused to glance at Tinker, who was bent over the paper, frowning in the same effort that exercised Blake's mind. And twice he leant over the lad's shoulder to study the characters afresh.

But not the faintest glimmer of inspiration came to him. All through that evening the pair studied and probed in vain. It was nearly midnight when they ventured out again for food, and on their return they tumbled straight into bed. It had been a long day from the time they had left the Green Woman that morning in Marseilles almost a hundred miles as they had travelled by rail, though only about thirty as the crow flies. Nor could the previous night be said to have been exactly of a peaceful nature.

The surly proprietor of the lodging-house condescended to serve them coffee and rolls the next morning, so there was no need to venture out.

And as soon as they had disposed of the food they went at the puzzle once more. By this time Blake had taken up a pad of paper and pencil and had begun to make a series of classifications of the various things such numbers might be employed to represent.

He began, for instance, with weights and measures, including avoirdupois, jewellers' weights, measures of quantity and area and every possible side classification.

He rang the changes on mathematical symbols. He included astronomy, chemistry, physics and dynamics.

He did not forget the vast field of number codes —a subject in which he was an expert.

Following this there was the question of the six mysterious letters.

Were they independent or interdependent? Did they represent a word? If so, in what language? He was a good student of ancient as well as modern languages, but he could fit such a word as "Soktim" to none that had come into his learning.

He left that to take Tinker out for more food and a spell of exercise. They bought some French papers while they were out, but in none of the local sheets did he see anything about Gros Jean. Nor was there any hint that a hue and cry was out for two Catalanians.

When they returned they found that the maid had done the room, and since they had taken care to take out with them the few items they possessed they had no fear that anything had been investigated during their absence.

Locking the door once more they settled down to the job afresh, Blake determined that he would tear out of those baffling letters and figures some sort of meaning. For he felt more and more convinced that they had an important bearing on the secret he was trying to probe, and which, since the events in Marseilles, he was more determined to uncover than ever before.

The figures danced before him. They became jumbled up with the letters in a mad confusion, sorting themselves into various forms which told him absolutely nothing.

He found himself repeating them over and over in different ways, speaking unconsciously, half aloud.

"Twenty-eight, thirty-eight, thirty-eight, twenty-eight—Soktim."

Just like that, first one way then another, until Tinker, despite the urgency of the matter, could not refrain from grinning.

"Sounds as if you were counting so much and then 'socking him,' guv'nor," he said, when Blake had been muttering for many minutes.

"I know. Can't you think of something more intelligent?"

Tinker subsided while Blake began again:

"Twenty-eight, thirty-eight —thirty-eight, twenty-eight —

twenty-eight —"

Suddenly Tinker looked up.

"I say, guv'nor."

"Well?"

"Sounds a little bit as if you were heaving the lead and calling the fathoms."

Blake stared at him frowningly, then all at once his face cleared. He jumped up and reached for his peasant's cap.

"Not so bad —not so bad! I've got an idea, young 'un. Your remark put something into my mind."

"What is it, guv'nor?"

"Never mind now. Wait here. I am going out, but I shall not be many minutes."

Before Tinker could question him further he was gone. But he was back again in a short time, and when he laid his purchase on the table Tinker saw that it was a second-hand chart of the eastern hemisphere.

Taking up his pencil once more, Blake ran it down the chart, using Greenwich as a starting point.

"Thirty-eight degrees south latitude, young 'un," he said as the pencil paused. "Now we'll follow it to twenty-eight degrees longitude east. That's about it —there. Do you see? The point of the pencil is on a spot among the Dodecanese Islands in the Aegean Sea. Only a few of them are named on the chart, but I know quite a number of them. Give me that paper again."[1]

He was betraying a rare excitement as he drew the paper towards him, and Tinker began to feel the same sense of thrill. He watched eagerly while Blake wrote the letters of the word beneath, transposing them this way and that like a word "chaotic" puzzle until suddenly he began to put them down in a quick certain way. And Tinker read:

MITKOS.

Blake threw the pencil down and lit a fresh caporal.

"There you are, Tinker. The island of Mitkos is certainly one of the Dodecanese group. They belong to Italy. I've never been on Mitkos. I believe it is privately owned. I seem to have heard that

---

[1] A keen student, with the internet on hand might notice that the references are somewhat off. The Aegean Sea is not a 'latitude south', but north and the longitude puts us 100 km inside Turkey. /drf

somewhere, though I can't be certain. But I know the name has come up in one way or another. Of course, it is only a guess that it lies that equivalent of longitude and latitude, but it can't be far off the mark. If so, what does it mean? Why should the latitude of that island be the same as the pass-word of the gang we are up against, Mitkos, Mitkos; let me think."

Tinker watched him while he resumed his pacing. Now that Blake had stated his theory it all seemed so simple. And so it was —to state it in simple terms after the key had been found.

But had it been found? Were there not other things, quite as suggestive, which could be made to fit those two numbers and that jumble of letters?

Studying them, Tinker saw that Mitkos was nothing more than Soktim written backwards. Neither form was English; one, at least, was Greek.

Did any language have such a word as, say, Kismot, or Mistok, or Miostk? That latter looked a bit Russian, he told himself.

Yet each time he came back to the fact that the different items did fit in with Blake's solution. There was an island of Mitkos, and it was situated at a point where the twenty-eighth degree of longitude east met the thirty-eighth degree of latitude south; or near enough as not to matter.

But what did it mean beyond that? Why should that figure, indicating the latitude of such a place, be used as a code-word by a bunch of dope sellers? Was the answer to be found on the island of Mitkos?

And this is exactly the question that Sexton Blake was also asking himself. The answer he found was communicated to Tinker, when, finally, he tossed the end of his cigarette away and sat down.

"We shall get on the move again, young 'un. We shall start this very night."

"Where are we going, guv'nor?"

"To Port Said —firstly."

"And after?"

"To the Island of Mitkos."

CHAPTER 9. At Port Said.

FOR nearly forty years a gloomy-looking ship chandlery has held its own against the encroachment of the spread of more modern buildings in a certain side street just off the waterfront at the eastern end of Port Said.

And for the same length of time the same sign, now so faded and begrimed that one can scarcely decipher the original lettering, has hung above the entrance.

If one pauses while the light is good one may slowly spell out:

F. H LLO AN

and if one takes the trouble to fill in the blanks one will come to the conclusion that the completed name had been minted "Halloran"; a surmise which would have been correct as anyone belonging to Port Said or, in fact, to any port of the Near or Far East could have explained.

There were few seafaring men who had ever passed through the Suez Canal who did not know or know of Fergus Halloran. Nor was that knowledge confined to a narrow passing back and forth. The yellow visaged, hook-nosed old rascal with a head as bald as an egg was spoken of in every part of the globe; and, mostly, the terms were not complimentary. Though why this should be so is not easy to understand, for any mariner who ever bought ships' gear from him had never had cause to complain about quality or price.

It was, rather, the sense of mystery that hung about Halloran. His repute was good or bad, depending on how one looked at things. It was said that there hadn't been a messy pot of intrigue in Egypt for forty years that he hadn't stirred. It was whispered that he had made many thousands out of the Moslem pilgrims that took their toilsome way to Mecca, shipping them in iron ships that blistered them beneath the sun, feeding them on maggoty scraps that would have given a camel the heebie-jeebies, dosing them with water that would have rusted the tubes of a Glasgow boiler.

There was loose talk, too, about the part he had played in the various upheavals in the Balkans, in Turkey, in Russia. There were those who swore by all their gods that Fergus Halloran knew more about gun-running than any pirate in the Red Sea or Persian Gulf.

It was said further that he held the secrets of the whole of the Near East in that yellow dome of his and that he had put away fabulous sums of money which he was too mean to invest even in gilt-edged securities.

Strange was it, then, that this man should be found always at his dingy place of business in Port Said. If he took a personal part in one tenth of the plots which he was credited as having fomented, he would have needed half a dozen astral bodies to project into space.

Nevertheless, there must have been something behind all the whispering, for many strange persons sought him out from time to time, and always, following such visits, events began to move in different quarters.

To see him and to transact ordinary business with him one would think, however, that his chandlery business occupied all his time and thought.

The stock was as comprehensive as possible. And it was of the best quality whether new or second-hand. Halloran had no use for useless junk. That was why, whether he was liked or not, mariners came back to him again and again. They knew they could depend during a dirty gale on any gear that Halloran had supplied.

It was an amazing jumble of stuff that one came upon in the gloom of the interior. Everything appertaining to ships was there, from a two-inch cotter pin to an anchor that would hold the Majestic; from a bit of carpenter's twine to a coil of six-inch manila; from candles to every variety of brass lantern; compasses and chronometers in every variety, sextants, parallels and what-not.

Everything seemed to be thrown higgledy-piggledy about the place. It would strike the ordinary observer, entering for the first time, that only sheer chance would bring forth what one desired. Yet let him but ask for any item, and, out of the depths of the gloom, would appear a gigantic Nubian who would fumble about for a few moments and then produce the exact article required. His method of stock keeping might be primitive, but it was as efficient as any loose-leaf system ever invented.

Halloran himself rarely appeared in the outer shop though he was readily available when asked for. Usually he sat in his little cubby hole of a back room poring over his books or examining strange-looking objects which were quickly thrust out of sight when a knock came at the door. Those furtive movements were about the only outward sign that there might be some truth in the strange rumours surrounding him.

To this place, then, came two individuals late one afternoon. The shadows were long across Egypt. Dusk was climbing up out of the Indian Ocean and soon would sweep across the sands that bordered the Canal, to turn the Mediterranean to a deeper purple, to black.

The street in which the ship chandlery was situated was almost deserted. The great warehouses which jostled it were closed for the day. Only a gate lantern showed here and there, ready for the coming of darkness. Nor was the light which gleamed through the dirty windows of the ship chandlery much brighter, though it was needed badly enough in that gloomy interior, which was shadowy even at midday.

These two persons walked as those who had come this way before. They ware dressed after the fashion of ordinary seamen, though their skins were so dark that one would not have classed them as British or any other Nordic race. At a glance one would have said they were Spanish or Portuguese.

They were, needless to say, Sexton Blake and Tinker. They had landed in Port Said only an hour or so before, and now Blake was paying this visit to Fergus Halloran to arrange, if possible, what he would need for the next step in his mission.

He and Halloran knew each other intimately. They had had many dealings together in the past, though they had not always been allies. There had been times when they had been pitted against each other in a deadly duel, and if any man living could have told some of the truth about the yarns that were current about Halloran, that man was Sexton Blake.[2]

But despite the fact that they had been foes at times, they had a deep mutual respect for each other, and because Blake knew there was no one who could give him anything approaching the aid which Halloran could provide, if the spirit moved him, he was going to recruit that aid if possible.

On first entering the shop they saw no one. But when Blake clapped his hands lightly the same giant Nubian whom he had seen many a time before, loomed up from behind a great heap of cordage. He was moving sluggishly until Blake spoke to him in Egyptian Arabic.

"Your master, is he in his private room?"

"He is in his room, effendi, but is seeing no one."

---

[2] Example, 'The Riddle of the Russian Gold' /drf

"He will see me," responded Blake curtly. "Go to him and say that an effendi from London whom he knows well wishes speech with him. Go—the matter is urgent."

The black turned and passed between two high piles of material. Blake would not have hesitated to reveal his identity had the man still hesitated, for the fellow knew him of old, and, on his part, Blake knew he would sooner die than betray Halloran.

He was back within a few moments, gesturing for Blake to follow him. He obeyed, Tinker keeping close at his heels. They found the chandler seated at his desk just as they had seen him the last time they had visited the place. He might have been clad in the same soiled suit of white; it might even have been the same quid of tobacco in his cheek.

He turned his head as they entered and took one brief glance. They had a feeling that even had he not suspected their identity he would have been able to pierce the disguise in that single stare.

He did not speak until the Nubian had retired. But then he motioned to the only other chair that the room boasted.

"Sit down, Blake," he said in a voice that was extraordinarily low and musical. "Find a place on that pile of books, Tinker. What brings you out to Egypt all dolled up like a couple of dagos?"

Both Blake and Tinker laughed and shook hands. Then they sat down.

"I'm on some business," admitted Blake. "And I've come to you for some information and some assistance."

"You seem to feel pretty certain I can give you both."

"You can if you feel inclined."

There was a brief silence. Halloran was going over in his mind all recent events in Egypt that might give him the key to Blake's presence without his having to ask. Blake was wondering what Halloran would say when he spoke the name "Mitkos."

He knew there was no lie in the rumours that Halloran had been mixed up in all sorts of intrigue and gun running. He suspected he might even know a good deal about the slave traffic of the Persian Gulf. But he did not believe the other had ever had a finger in the accursed pie that was concocted of illicit drugs. The figures given at a recent meeting of the League of Nations in Geneva were sufficient to indicate the appalling proportions of the traffic.

"What do you want to know?" asked Halloran at last.

"What do you know about the Island of Mitkos in the Dodecanese group in the Aegean?"

Halloran's pale blue eyes fixed Blake in a profound stare.

"What the devil has put that into your head?"

"Then you do know something about it."

"Enough to warn you, in confidence, to leave it alone."

"Ah! That sounds interesting. Just what is this island? Somehow the name is familiar to me, but I can't recall in what way."

"You probably heard it mentioned or read about it about four years ago. It was mentioned at the time of the Greek evacuation of Smyrna."

A light came into Blake's eyes.

"I've got it now. You have given me just the hint I needed. If I recall the incident correctly, there was some controversy as to whom it belonged."

"Exactly. Greece claimed it. Italy claimed it. And Turkey flirted with the same idea. It stands at that point of the Dodecanese where the Italian, Greek and Turkish lines meet in the water. It is, in fact, right on the line. There was some error in the survey that gave the group to Italy. The matter isn't settled yet. Turkey has dropped out, but Italy and Greece still claim rights. But neither interferes with it. It wouldn't do them any good if they did."

"Why?"

"Because it has been in the hands of the same family of overlords for centuries. It is a sort of petty kingdom. There aren't many people on it, but the present over-lord, like his predecessors, keeps feudal state. And you can take it from me he is a tough nut to crack —if that is in your mind."

"Just who is he?"

"His name is Stefan Goupolis."

"The deuce! I know the fellow. I have seen him on the Riviera and in Paris."

"No doubt. He gets around a bit when he isn't locked away on his island."

"He is rich?"

"He'd give Ford a run for first place."

"Inherited?"

"Now, now, Blake, you are getting too pressing. How do I know where it came from? I can tell you that the island is as strong and modern a fortress as any first-class nation could make it. He's got a full sized steam yacht, a peach of a sailing schooner, a useful motor cruiser and other craft as well. I understand he has an aeroplane and all sorts of other luxuries —his own wireless station for example."

"He seems to be a high roller."

"He is —so high you'd better not try and bring him down."

"You seem to hold him in considerable respect."

"His power —yes."

"Doesn't he do anything to employ his wealth profitably?"

Halloran wagged a finger at Blake.

"No, you don't, my friend. That is the second trap you have laid for me inside five minutes. I'm saying no more. But I repeat my advice —leave him alone."

"We'll leave that for the moment," responded Blake with a smile. "I want you to get hold of a small but seaworthy craft for me. How soon can it be managed?"

"Where are you going?"

"Just for a bit of a cruise."

"Give me particulars of what you want."

For answer, Blake thrust a hand inside his coat and took out an envelope.

"I've got them all ready, Halloran. Here they are."

"I'll go into them to-night, and let you know to-morrow morning. Will that do?"

"Quite well. I should want full equipment and stores."

"I'll give you a round figure to cover everything."

"Splendid. And now can you suggest where Tinker and I should stay to-night? I don't want to risk being recognised in Port Said."

"If you want to lie really doggo you can have one of the lofts above this. It is plain but clean and furnished for sleeping. It has been used for that before."

"I accept most gratefully."

"I'd take you home, but I have a meeting there to-night. Hassan will look after you all right and can manage what food you will want."

The arrangements suited Blake well enough. Only by the favour of Lady Luck and steady, heavy bribery had he and Tinker succeeded in getting along the Mediterranean without being spotted. He had no desire to run any unnecessary risks now, after having gained so much;

and he knew pretty well the sort of people with whom Halloran would be having a conference.

Blake didn't need any telling that this job on which he and the lad were engaged was as big a two-handed proposition as they had ever tackled. Yet he knew he could not yet ask for any official assistance. Until he got real, vital proof, it was essential for him to follow a lone trail.

He would get out of Halloran more about the mysterious Stefan Goupolis, but he knew sufficient already to warn him that every step was dangerous.

Blake's instinct told him that Goupolis was very, very close to the top of the tree. There might be others still more powerful; or he might have confederates who were co-equal.

But the more he learned, in small scraps, about the island of Mitkos, the more his instinct told him it was there he would find the answer to the riddle.

He anticipated far greater difficulties than he had tackled. But his wildest imaginings could not have foreseen just what he and Tinker were to plunge into.

Halloran contented himself with advising Blake to drop his aim, whatever it might be. When he saw that Blake was not to be swerved from his course, he laid himself out to fulfil his requirements.

The craft eventually chosen was a forty foot sailing dhow that could be handled by four men. This meant Halloran had to find two of a crew who would be trustworthy, and this he achieved by producing a pair of ruffians who had served in some of his own mysterious jobs in the Red Sea and Persian Gulf.

Three days hence, Blake and Tinker came out of hiding. The two ruffians provided by Halloran were no 'tougher' in appearance than they.

Their disguise was that of Levantine sailormen, and for the better part of two days Blake had worked with infinite patience to ensure that they would pass muster under any possible complication of conditions.

The stain which he had applied had been carried to every portion of the body. Not even prolonged immersion in salt water would have any effect on it.

Hassan had procured a hair dye from the famous, ancient Nubian prescription that had been used since the time of Cleopatra.

Tiny rubber rings, thrust far up the nostrils, had given a broad effect to their noses while their garments had been chosen by Halloran himself.

It would be easy enough for Blake to get along with the argot of the coast but, in Tinkers case, it had been thought wiser to fix on him a character somewhat like that he had adopted back in Barcelona. In this instance, though, he posed as a Greek Levantine who had spent some time in America, for he had a perfect command of the 'dago' slang of the New York East Side and waterfront.

On the third morning they took leave of Halloran. That individual shook a pessimistic head over the whole business, sucking his cigar noisily as he drawled:

"Maybe I can guess what you're up to; and then, again, maybe I can't. But if you take my advice, Blake, you'll leave it alone."

Blake matched his shrug.

"It's not trampling on your toes, is it?"

"No; I wouldn't touch it with a ten foot pole. This is one stunt from which I don't think you'll come back."

"Well, if not, there'll be rejoicing in gangland."

"There must be a big thing behind it," soliloquised Halloran. "I'll give you a final tip before you go —though I shouldn't. That bird, Goupolis, is called the Black Magician among the islands. I don't know, how he got the name or what sort of black magic he indulges in. But I do know he is a tough nut to crack. Keep your eyes peeled."

"Much obliged. I had already made up my mind that he was resourceful. I'll let you know how things turn out —when we get back."

"I won't live long enough for that," grunted Halloran.

With a final wave of the hand, Blake started off towards the waterfront. Dawn, pink and pearly, was just mounting out of the Red Sea. At the entrance to the Canal, a big Australian liner was edging into the strip of water while a dingy little tramp was poking her nose out of that link with the East.

Along the waterfront of Port Said were scores and scores of all sorts of craft, from stately P. & O. mailboats to rakish little dhows no larger than that in which Blake and Tinker were venturing.

The bumboats were already swarming about the passenger ships. Up by the Hotel Europe, some white-clad tourists were sleepily surveying the sky as they prepared to make the journey to Cairo for the day, little dreaming that the two dirty looking Levantines who trudged past then in the dusty road were two London detectives bound on as dangerous a job as would have set them gaping even wider had they known the truth.

Blake and Tinker found the crew of two already in the boat. The setting of their feet on the deck seemed to be a signal to the wind god, for at that moment the water began to ripple under a fresh morning breeze and, soon after, in common with other sailing dhows, they found the blue Mediterranean singing under their bows.

Once they were clear of Port Said and had left Damietta off to port, Blake, who had taken control of the long tiller, steered a course almost exactly north-west.

Continued, this would bring them right in among the islands of the Dodecanese, but it was his intention, if all went well, to alter his course at the end of the second day in order to skirt the lower, south-east islands of the group —thus passing fairly close to the eastern point of Crete.

Not that it mattered to him whether he found himself in Greek, Italian or Turkish waters. His aim was to keep, as far as possible, in free waters and to make his base as nearly as could be to the island that was his objective —Mitkos.

That, of course, could be regarded as no-man's island unless it were taken to be the private domain of Stefan Goupolis. But Blake was satisfied that, whatever methods he might use to approach Mitkos, he would not be violating the laws of any of the three countries referred to.

If the present wind held he figured on being off Crete by the evening of the second day. And the Red Sea Arabs who formed the crew, Ali and Ben-abi, agreed with him that all the signs pointed to a steady spell.

Whether these two picturesque ruffians had any private curiousity as to his identity or purpose one couldn't tell. They went about their duties with scarcely a word. One of them appointed himself cook and managed astonishingly well.

They knew their work, had no criticism to make that the small craft was undermanned for such a long voyage, accepted both Blake and Tinker at their face value, and seemed more than content with the wages they were receiving.

What Halloran had said to them, Blake couldn't guess. But that they were completely under his domination was plain. And a more blood-thirsty looking couple it would have been difficult to dig up in Port Said. Blake thought, privately, that they would possibly prefer to be engaged on some piratical cruise in the Persian Gulf; but, if that were so, it did not cause them to loaf on the present job.

It seemed, at last, as if their brief spell of luck was to hold, for they raised the light on Cape Sidera almost to the hour on which Blake had counted, and by dawn the following morning were off Sares.

It was that same evening that they slid into a little bay on the island of Myros— his secondary objective.

There was nothing odd in the appearance of their dingy craft in that harbour. Myros is a point of call for most of the inter-island trade of the Aegean. The vessels from every port of Greece and Asia Minor as well as from the different islands of the Cyclades and the Dodecanese, put in there at one time or another. It is, too, almost on the direct route between Constantinople and Port Said and, for sailing craft on that voyage, a convenient port of call.

And here, for the next five days, Blake and Tinker lay low, living aboard their craft, mixing little with the other sailor folk in port. But Ali and Ben-abi went ashore regularly, drinking (they were far from being strict Moslems) gossiping and, on one occasion, getting mixed up in a knife fight that might have proved embarrassing to Blake had he been in haste to depart.

That incident, as it turned out, served his purpose excellently. He had not proposed taking Ali and Ben-abi on the next leg of the journey. He had been planning to leave them at Myros to find a passage back to Port Said as best they could. That would not be difficult with so many boats leaving for that port; and he would see that they were well provided for.

But when he learned that, in common with half a dozen other rowdies, they had been pushed into the local gaol, he delayed paying their fines as requested.

Down below he and Tinker discussed the matter.

"What will you do about it, guv'nor?" asked the lad, cautious even in the security of the odoriferous cabin.

"This suits our book right down to the ground, young 'un —if we can keep them in there until the storm breaks."

"Well, the sky looks threatening enough."

"And the glass has fallen with a thud. If we could haul out of here this afternoon we might make Mitkos before dark. But, as I said, we want to arrive there as if driven in by the storm."

"Then why don't you start, guv'nor? You could send the money to them at the last moment."

"I think that is just what we will do, my lad. And now —mind your tongue while we are on deck."

He led the way up the short companion and stood studying the black clouds that were piling up in the south-west. By all the signs of sky as well as barometer, a nasty storm was brewing, and it had been for just one of these seasonal blows that Blake had been waiting during the past five days.

He had no excuse for sailing into Mitkos harbour in fine weather. It was privately owned —was not a trading port —and all its sea services were handled by the personal craft of the overlord.

That much and quite a lot more he had picked up in Myros. But if they were to reach the harbour at Mitkos in the teeth of a heavy blow, it would appear but a normal chance of the sea. Even Stefan Goupolis, Blake figured, could hardly be suspicious of two dhow seamen arriving on his island in that fashion.

He knew they would be liable to close examination. But he was not fearing that. He wanted to reach Mitkos, was determined to reach Mitkos, and could figure no better way of doing so.

All along, he had realised what a danger to that plan Ali and Ben-abi would be. Therefore he had determined to leave them behind in Myros.

But now they seemed to have solved that difficulty themselves. If they should remain in gaol until he got away, they could believe that he was angry with them, which would serve quite well.

As the inky blackness of the storm clouds seemed to deepen to an even greater intensity, he wagged his head in decision.

"Remain here," he muttered to Tinker. "I'll go ashore and fix things up. We'll leave as soon as I get back."

Half an hour later Tinker saw his tall figure coming hastily along the rough beach, watched while he jumped into a small boat and pulled himself out to the dhow.

Already the surface of the tiny, landlocked harbour was stirring restlessly, as if some giant subterranean hand were moving beneath the surface, clutching at it from far out to sea.

The storm clouds were so closely packed now that the scudding sections could not be distinguished. An ominous calm had settled over everything; the whitewashed huts of the village reflected back a strange yellow. The sea birds were swooping and screaming uneasily. All the signs of a nasty storm lay overhead, and the lad began to wonder if they would need to make any bluff of being driven ashore by the time they reached Mitkos —if they ever made it.

But that seemed not to worry Blake as he sprang aboard. He had already told Tinker that it would be just as well if he remained at Port Said, had repeated the offer at Myros —but Tinker had shown such indignation at the suggestion that he did not repeat it.

Nor did he tell him now that all the talk in the town was of an exceptionally bad blow coming on. The lad would see for himself how the hands on the other craft in the harbour were snugging things down in readiness.

For the last three hours other boats had been making this haven from outside; one or two were still trying to beat in between the heads.

Every seaman's eye in the place would stare in amazement at any craft venturing out in the teeth of an oncoming storm such as was threatening.

And, indeed, in another half hour, when the dhow went lurching across the harbour and rolled sluggishly through the heads just as a low moaning sound broke over the whole visible world, men back in the town spat and murmured at the madness of the man who leaned against the tiller.

But Blake and Tinker had no time for that. Almost as soon as they were clear of the harbour a long line of white came rushing towards them, the moaning turned to a roaring sound that filled all their world.

Then they were standing at a steep angle as the old dhow shivered under the impact of the hammering assault of the storm.

CHAPTER 10.   The Storm.

AN appalling darkness blotted out everything.

It was, on the face of it, sheer madness for those two to start out in the teeth of such an upheaval of nature.

Yet Sexton Blake had weighed the risks against the possibility of gaining his ends.

It was not only a case as a case that had driven him so far through difficulties that, time and again, had threatened to cut short not only his efforts but career and life as well.

There was, in his present spirit, something of the urge of the crusaders of old. It had not been the tactful approach of certain persons high in international authority that had decided him to prosecute this campaign against the vile beings who lurked behind the terrible net that was tripping thousands of victims.

It was not the prospect of material gain or enhancement of fame that caused him to accept the gauge.

Rather was it the pitiful sight of that girl whom he had carried out of the dive in Soho. To Blake she had meant more than just one victim of the scourge. She represented all those poor wretches who had been dragged beneath the wheels of the terrible juggernaut — Dope.

In his mind was a vision. Faces, on which had been painted every phase of human agony, swam in a vast sea that was engulfing the unseen bodies in their thousands. Yet as rapidly as the monster swallowed them up others were swept into his ken, hesitating, resurging, retreating, floating ever nearer to the abyss that disappeared into impenetrable blackness beyond.

From every clime those doomed creatures came. Over every land hung the shadow of the monstrous net that lured them to their doom. Of every race and colour and creed were the lost.

And above, smooth, sleek, smiling, ghoulishly triumphant, sat the evil ones who fattened and battened on the ruin of their fellows.

That was the vision that haunted him; that was the vision that carried him on against all odds to seek out and attack the fountain-head of the ghastly traffic.

Was Mitkos the heart of the great conspiracy?

He did not know —yet.

Was Stefan Goupolis one of these seated at the pinnacle?

He had not yet the answer to that.

Would he rend asunder a vital part of the fabric if he dragged down Goupolis?

The answer might lie beyond that terrific storm.

And it seemed that all the forces of Nature had been summoned to drive him back, to say him nay.

It was more like the frantic burst of the Indian monsoon, more the fury of the China Coast typhoon than a storm of the more temperate Mediterranean.

Its intensity was tropical; its violence was cosmic. It seemed, time and again, that the little dhow (which was really more of a gulf pattimar than anything else) would stand, literally, on her tail and somersault. It appeared impossible that she could weather the incredible violence that was assailing her.

Outwardly she appeared ill suited for such an attempt. Dingy, awkward in line with her clumsily-raked mast and her low freeboard, she looked an easy victim for the first big sea that struck her. Yet, in some miraculous way, she came nose down to it after each appalling heave, then she seemed to dive bottom-wards in a smother of water and foam, through a shrieking hullaballoo that deafened the two who clung to the long tiller and tore into shredded echoes the one yell that Tinker essayed.

Mitkos lay sixteen miles almost due east of Myros. On a clear day one could see it from a high point on the latter, though Mitkos snuggled so close to the bosom of the sea that it appeared but a low smudge against the horizon.

That was the only reckoning Blake had to go on. Nor could he even use Myros now as a stern mark, for it had been smothered from sight by the storm.

Would they strike their mark even if the dhow remained afloat? Child of the storm —that was all she was. Would she be swirled upon that one dot that lay ahead, or would they be rushed past it, swept into the inferno of tiny, rocky islets farther on, just as those myriad faces of Blake's vision were swallowed by the terrible abyss?

They could not even profess to guide the craft. All that was possible was to hang on to the long tiller and wait, hoping that the rag of a sail would not be torn utterly to ribbons.

A mad thing, but a glorious attempt.

With the full force of the tempest almost directly behind them, it was obvious that they were sweeping along at a terrific rate. Now and then, during one of those moments when the elements took a breath for renewed effort, they could catch a glimpse of heaving, storm-tossed waters ahead on every side.

Behind them came rushing, gigantic waves that threatened to engulf them, batter them flat against the hissing, furious surface on which they rode.

But again and again they lifted, rose to dizzying heights, only to plunge down at an angle and speed that switchbacked them violently up another slope.

Over the tiller they retched, nauseated by the agony of that pitching and cavorting. Outraged stomach and diaphragm were protesting in the only way Nature made possible.

But Sexton Blake hung on no more grimly than the lad. Tinker had absorbed something of the spirit that was driving the elder. His part had, as of necessity, been a subordinate one.

Yet he had been ready enough to strike when the moment came, as witness the speed and precision with which he had smashed Gros Jean back at the Silver Tower in Marseilles.

Blake had lost count of time. That driving, lashing chaos of the elements hammered all calculations from his brain. It beat down upon him so heavily as to numb his faculties —all but that spark of determination to reach his goal.

It might have been minutes since they slid out from the yellow glare of Myros; it might have been hours that they had been careering across this heaving world.

Mitkos might lie far, far behind them. At any moment they might crash upon the rocks of the islets beyond. They might even drive between them and find a last resting-place on the mainland of Asia Minor.

Yet still, as mortal man will, he clung to the tiller, a feeble speck in that tearing chaos about him.

And then, somewhere behind them, the veil of smother split asunder. For a few brief moments a wondrous glory of light and promise was born from the centre of the storm.

It cut the veil like a cosmic sword, revealing a shimmering pillar of flame that burned to pale silver and then deepened again to rose.

A weird play of reflection was thrown back from the streaming wall into which they were driving. Every drop of that drenching sky seemed to pick up the light and throw it back. And, as through a glass darkly, they saw, beyond, a shape.

Mitkos!

Blake yelled the word at the top of his lungs, but before it could travel even the short distance to where Tinker clung, it had been ripped away and tossed into the whirlpool of sound that beat about them.

But the lad had seen and knew.

Mitkos!

His lips, too, formed the word, and as the glow widened, deepened, grew until it stabbed the zenith, they looked at each other, peering beneath the straggling hair that drenched about their eyes, but seeing the glint of courage in each other's gaze.

Mitkos!

Was it so? Could it be so?

Behind them the wonder of the light was spreading with amazing swiftness. The storm was sweeping on into the upper Aegean, where it would be sucked through the chimney of the Dardanelles and spill into the Sea of Marmora, where it would batter itself against the jagged peaks of Stranja Dagh, and die, sobbing, in the Black Sea.

It was one of those miraculous tempests which the Mediterranean can produce —the hysterical scream of a woman, to come and go in a flash, or the deep-toned anger of the giant to lash in fury for days.

Mitkos!

They saw it as it lay sprawled right ahead of them.

Straight as Fate itself they sped towards the narrow entrance of the harbour. They could glimpse the roofs of the little village from which the water was still pouring in a thousand streamers; they could see the snowy white of the villa that stood alone against its background of intense green.

The house, the home, the lair of Stefan Goupolis. Was it the heart of the web? Was the spider at home?

Had it been possible for Blake and Tinker to send sight ahead and penetrate those walls even into the depths that lay beneath the visible portion they would have had an answer.

While the tempest raged overhead, Stefan Goupolis had remained in a world that knew not such sudden chaos.

From the comfort of a low chair in his sea garden room he had watched the deepening opaline of the water outside, had gazed with sensuous pleasure at the waving fronds in his garden that lay so snug and safe beneath the lashing fury of the surface.

That gentle waving was the only sign that storm was tearing the waters asunder; only that mild disturbance reached to the bed where his exotic blooms made riot of colour in their white and crimson setting.

Yet Stefan Goupolis knew well enough what the storm was like. He had seen the islands whipped and beaten too many times not to realise what a scythe of death followed in the wake of those sudden outbursts.

Yet he never dreamed that something of major interest to himself was speeding towards Mitkos in the cloud of smother. He was on the qui vive for a mysterious coming. That much warning he had received through the air. And he would be ready, he told himself.

From his secret agent in Marseilles he had had a warning that two strangers had been probing the organisation at Marseilles. He knew that something had happened at Barcelona. He knew of the affair at the Green Woman, and he had received a report about the attack on Gros Jean in the Silver Tower. But Gros Jean had been able to give no clue, for he still lay in bandages, forbidden to speak. Blake had not been wrong when he surmised that Gros Jean's skull would need to be trepanned.

Goupolis knew, too, that the same two mysterious persons had vanished as if from the face of the earth.

What had become of them? Would they, like the last fool who had gone to his fate in that terrible pool in the sea garden room, find their way to Mitkos?

If so he would be ready for them. Let them come. There were only two ways —by sea or by air.

He had a good look-out and a safe defence. He would know how to deal with them when they arrived. But they would never come through this storm. It was just one more shield that stood before Mitkos.

Nevertheless, no matter how safe he felt, he never neglected caution. At certain hours of the day he made it a point to inspect the various units of his compact organisation —to receive reports from his guards, to keep his finger very closely on the pulse of life within his little world.

Thus the duty he rose now to perform was one to which he

attended several times each day, and not inspired by the storm or anything that might come out of it.

He walked leisurely to the curved wall of the sea garden room opposite the spot where a water-tight door gave entrance into the dock which housed the submarine.

Here a mirror-fronted panel, similar to the other, moved aside at his touch. He stepped into a small chamber, brilliantly lit by a cluster of bulbs in the centre of the ceiling, and having other brackets studded at different parts of the wall, so that, if necessary, the place could be illuminated to an intense whiteness.

Almost the whole interior was fitted with tables and boards to which were affixed gleaming brass instalments, knobs, levers, slots, and what-not, or black vulcanite gadgets akin to the other fitments.

There was a large, mahogany cabinet, like a wireless-receiving apparatus, which, indeed, it was. There were sending keys through which he could communicate with his private aerial station in the village; there were vulcanite disks marked with abbreviated names and graduated with lines by the manipulation of which he could receive from any sending station in the world and on any wavelength.

There was a second large mahogany cabinet, the front panel being of ground glass, any direct glare being screened from it by a wide vulcanite "hood" that cowled the top and sides.

This, like the big receiver, was connected up with a fitted board, and it was in front of this that Stefan Goupolis now seated himself.

His hand sought a milled knob at one side of the box; then, with his other hand he switched off the cluster of lights, leaving the place in darkness except for a faint glow that came from some invisible source.

Almost at once a vision appeared on the ground glass in front of him. At first it was only a blurred mass of patches, but as he kept turning the knob to focus, a startlingly clear vision of trees and houses appeared, minute figures of humans moving about, steam jutting from a brick stack.

It was a simple television of his own village, and when he was satisfied with the industry this presented, he altered direction and focus to bring in a panorama that included the wireless sending mast, the white roof of the underground hangar and, finally, the little bay.

Even this sheltered spot was disturbed from the violence of the storm, but now the sun was shining low in the west, and as the focus lifted a little to reveal the twin headlands of the tiny bay, he saw something rising and falling on the heaving sea outside.

Stefan Goupolis frowned quickly and moved the milled knob very slowly to follow the course of this object. He could see that it was a small sailing craft, a pattimar such as was more common farther south than up in this part of the Aegean.

And it was obvious, from the ragged, storm-beaten appearance that it had gone through a bad pounding.

But what was it doing out at such a time? Why wasn't it in harbour? Why should it be heading for Mitkos? Was it being driven here by the storm? Mitkos was off the beaten track. Yet the wind had been terrific and might have blown it thither.

If that were so, then he would give the occupants shelter and send them away within a few hours. On the other hand, there was the warning —two mysterious persons, and all the television showed him of human beings on this almost derelict craft were two, clinging to the long tiller.

That enemy could only come in one of two ways —by air or by sea. Was this they arriving in the wake of the tempest, borne hither on its wings?

The doubt was sufficient to cause him to act. If he were wrong it did not matter. What were a couple of lives, more or less, against his safety? Against the inviolable sanctity of the organisation?

He put out his right hand and laid it on a polished brass lever. Then he waited, staring at the television plate until he saw the tossing chip of a craft come onwards towards the mouth of the harbour. Now it appeared to be almost opposite the twin heads; now it was rising high on the crest of a huge wave that would send it scudding down right inside the bay.

But although the wave broke and raced inwards, although the boat started to follow, it never reached its goal, for, while it still hung perched on an angle, Goupolis dragged back on the lever.

At once some invisible barrier seemed to rise up and catch the keel of the pattimar as it fell. It could be seen, even in the ground-glass plate, that it had struck hard, was quivering in a death agony before bucking upwards once more to crash a second time. Then it rolled over and over towards the curve of the beach, only a flashing glimpse of an arm showing that one, at least, of the occupants was making a fight for his life.

Stefan Goupolis pushed the lever back into place and resumed his watch on the glass. He smiled to himself as he saw the wreck of the dhow rolling sluggishly towards the shore. But he frowned as he made out a figure fighting valiantly through the water; and he cursed softly when he caught sight of still a second survivor headed in the same direction.

Swiftly he pushed his hand towards one of the sending keys. He tapped out a quick, brief message to the village station which was a command that would soon be spread among his men. None were to go near the beach without his orders.

All the time he had been watching the drama being played out on the ground-glass screen, and one might have heard, had one been present, a sibilant hiss of anger as he watched two figures drag themselves out of the water and, after staggering a few feet up the sandy beach, drop in exhaustion.

One of them, the taller, rolled over and made what seemed to be an effort to reach his companion; but he collapsed after covering a few feet, and, after a convulsive jerking of the body, lay quite still.

Only then did Stefan Goupolis switch on the lights once more.

CHAPTER 11.   The House of Curtains.

JUST an infinitesimal fraction of a moment before they struck, Blake knew it was no natural obstruction that was to break the dhow's back.

Something in the penetrating power of the angled light, or in some quality of the water, gave him one swift glance of a massive steel arm just beneath the surface of the water.

Then they smashed full on to it.

There was no time to prepare. There was no chance to warn the lad of what he had seen. Before even he could do more than brace himself —and he had only relaxed his pose for a few seconds as they mounted to the top of the inrushing wave —they were pounding on to the unyielding barrier of steel.

To both him and Tinker it seemed that the boat made a clean somersault after striking the second time. They had a confused sensation of being pitched over and over in a smother of foam and water, and then of being sucked down and down and down, until it seemed their lungs must burst.

It was Tinker's arm which Stefan Goupolis had glimpsed for one brief moment as the boat pitched inwards; but it was Blake whom he saw next, fighting his way shorewards.

But, as Goupolis was told by his television cabinet, Tinker was not far behind, and, again, it was Blake who, after falling flat on his face through sudden shock and exhaustion, struggled up and made one strenuous but futile effort to reach the lad.

Thus they lay, two bits of flotsam tossed up on that unfriendly, dangerous beach. None came near them. Goupolis' people in the village did not even peer curiously from afar. They knew better than to disobey the mandate of their overlord, even had they felt inclined to do so.

Nor did Goupolis seem to bother further about them after switching off the television. From the sea-garden room he ascended in the tiny lift to the ground floor of the villa, and there he entered a small room which was fitted with instrument boards, levers, knobs, and other gadgets much after the fashion of the one he had just left. But it served a very diffcrent purpose, as Blake and Tinker were soon to discover.

The exhaustion that held the two detectives was not that of a protracted period of strain. It was the cumulative effect of mental and physical shock, and receded under the natural stimulus of the reserve forces which Blake and Tinker, like all thoroughly fit people, possess.

It was, in fact, Tinker who recovered first; though it was he who had been sunk deepest in the grip of oblivion.

The afternoon sun was shining warmly on him when he opened his eyes and, rolling over, saw Blake. Getting to his feet slowly, but with ever-increasing strength, he tottered across to where Blake lay.

Kneeling down he laid a hand on Blake's shoulder. Blake muttered something and rolled on his back, his closed eyes full to the sky.

Tinker shook him again.

"Guv'nor! Are you all right?"

Blake's lids lifted and he sat up.

"What the —oh, I remember! How do you feel, young 'un? I thought you were all in."

"I've swallowed half the ocean, and I feel as if I'd been beaten with a thousand sticks, but I'm all right, guv'nor."

"I feel about the same. The boat is finished."

Tinker pointed farther along the beach, where the dhow, now only a mass of wreckage, rolled in the gentle swell that reached her.

"We'll never leave in her, guv'nor. I don't understand what we struck. It was like —"

"Like hitting a steel barrier, which is exactly what happened to us, young 'un," interrupted Blake.

"What on earth do you mean?" asked the lad, agape.

"Just what I say. Strangers are not welcome on this island, which, I presume, is Mitkos, whether they come in fair weather or foul. I had just time to catch a glimpse of an enormous steel bar across the mouth of the bay before we struck it; a devilish mechanical contrivance, but an effective one."

He stood up and gazed about him. Over a clump of trees a plume of smoke was rising.

"There are people over there, Tinker. I wonder if we were seen. Or is that barrier kept down all the time. I think we had better do a little exploring. But, first, let me have a look at you."

He scrutinised the lad carefully, nodding his head slowly from moment to moment.

"Your disguise hasn't suffered much. It is a good thing I

anticipated we might have a rough passage. How is mine?"

"I can't see anything wrong, guv'nor."

"Well, listen carefully, Tinker! We don't know yet that this is Mitkos. We might have been driven miles past it. But I've a hunch that we have struck it —that steel barrier. Anyway, we'll investigate. So watch your step, every moment; don't forget the part you are playing. Do you feel ready to go forward?"

"Sure, guv'nor, I'm ready!"

"Then come on!"

They had gone less than twenty yards when they caught sight of the wireless tower; then, as they turned half right, they saw the lovely white villa set amidst the mass of green. Had Blake had any doubts about whether this was Mitkos, they vanished now.

"We've hit it," he muttered in a low lone. "Can't tell who may be spying or what methods they may use. Careful, young 'un. We'll make direct for the house."

As they reached a sort of path they caught a fleeting glimpse of the cottages in the village, but instead of proceeding in that direction, Blake led the way to the right, which would, he figured, take them up to the villa.

About two hundred yards farther on they saw a turning to the left, and this was so well made and graded that they were not surprised when they reached a stone gateway, which lcd to the first of the carefully-tended terraces.

Now they could see the whole stretch of the white colonnaded piazza, though of any human being they saw no sign. Yet the wide doors and windows were thrown open to the soft air, and there were, on every side, as well as about the house, a multitude of signs that the place was lived in and that the master was now in residence.

A strange pair they made as they walked up the path, mounted short flights of steps, and on along the path again —swarthy, their patchy garments sodden from immersion in the sea, their hair tangled from the whipping of the gale, their Port Said shoes squelching water at every step.

Shipwrecked mariners never presented a greater picture of forlorn need than this pair who had arrived on Mitkos in such dramatic manner. And their bedraggled appearance was the greater in contrast with the trim lawns on either side and that snowy villa above.

It would not have surprised Blake if a pack of dogs had come tearing down the path to rend them into worse tatters; nor if men-servants with clubs had rushed out to drive them away.

But nothing happened. Neither man nor beast gave sign of living. Only that plume of smoke back at the village showed that some life was stirring in this strange place.

It was uncanny, in a way. It was sinister, despite the warm sun that shone on their backs. It was menacing.

They paused at the bottom of the wide steps that led to the piazza. Now they could see along the whole stretch of its flooring, which was just about shoulder high.

And at one spot was further evidence of occupation.

There stood a small table with an immaculate cloth. There were bits of delicate china and silver, a silver lamp and kettle.

There was a covered silver muffin dish, a book open face down on a long, comfortable cane chair —tea waiting for someone, and the book suggesting that he would be there at any moment.

Blake started up the steps with Tinker beside him. At the top he paused again. Not a sound. He made a tapping sound on the wood floor with his foot, thinking to attract the attention of a servant.

No one came.

They were standing just opposite the wide-open front doors of the house and, through this, could see the beautifully fluted pillars that supported the roof of the spacious interior.

It was one of the most architecturally beautiful buildings of its sort that Blake had ever gazed upon. It was as if it had been brought bodily from a grove of ancient Greece, where an Oracle had held court. It was more than that. It was temple, palace, auditorium, in one.

With a sign to Tinker to wait where he was, he ventured across the piazza and rapped on one of the doors. The sound echoed along through the vista of pillars until it seemed to die away in the gloom beyond.

He waited for some moments. No one came. Again he rapped, this time adding his voice in a call, phrased in modern Greek.

Voice and echo of knuckles were lost, as before. He made a sign for Tinker to join him.

"We've come so far we'll go on," he whispered. "Keep close to me. I don't like the look of this, and yet there is nothing —"

He stepped over the threshold and, in doing so, penetrated one of the greatest puzzles of all his career. Tinker kept close beside him.

Blake thought he could see straight ahead between the miniature forest of pillars, another door. He would open that and see whither it might lead, he told himself.

Two rows of the pillars seemed to form a sort of aisle, and along this way he strode.

Then, suddenly, with a smothered imprecation, he pulled up. He had no choice.

A heavy red curtain had swept across their passage, appearing, it seemed, from nowhere.

He frowned at it and shot a glance at Tinker. The lad was gazing back at him in stupefaction.

Warned that his uneasiness had been well-founded, Blake decided to retreat to the piazza. He gestured to Tinker and turned.

Another red curtain blocked their way.

Blake laid a hand on it and dragged it aside, telling himself that this bogey-man stuff was too childish. Whatever might be beyond, there could be no difficulty in regaining the veranda, for they had come only a few strides after stepping over the threshold.

But, on dragging the obstructing curtain aside, he gave vent to a fresh imprecation, for in front of them was still another.

Tinker touched his arm and motioned to their right. There hung still another curtain. He knew, without looking, that still a fourth barricaded the way to the left.

He stood perfectly still, his hand on the lad's arm. He looked behind them at deep red; he studied the soft, red walls on each side and in front. He peered upwards, to find that he could see nothing but a void. He got to his knees and felt the floor. It seemed to be of the same hard-wood blocks as he had noticed on entering.

Then, once more he faced the direction in which the piazza lay. Less than eight feet, at most, should separate them from the door and the outer air. Three good strides would carry them out of this Maskelyne stunt. It was silly, ridiculous to allow that odd sensation of panic to creep up on one when the whole outdoors was so close at hand.

Curtains were not bolts and bars and stone walls. It would only be necessary to drag this one, or perhaps two, aside, and there they would be.

Savagely he caught the cloth again and hauled it aside. Right ahead of them was another. Tinker, seeing his purpose, took hold of that. They found a fresh one hanging before them.

The odd part was that, enclosed though they now were in a sort of box, a faint light showed them their immediate surroundings. It came, Blake figured, from somewhere up above, reflected from the ceiling or upper part of the white pillars.

And the outer air must now be only five or six feet, for they had covered two short steps.

They tackled the curtain that now hung before them, and then drew a simultaneous breath of relief as they saw a clean yard of floor straight ahead of them.

They took it as one person. Their hands caught at the curtain and hauled it aside.

Before them was another full stride of floor with the same red barricade separating them from the piazza. To right and left were other curtains, and now, in the sudden relief he felt at the thought that this last curtain was all that separated them from their goal, Blake smiled grimly and looked back.

Then the smile vanished for, stretching away as they had come, was a dim vista with no curtains to obstruct them for a considerable distance. The half dozen or so they had dragged aside had vanished utterly.

Yet no pillar was in sight. The flexible, yielding sidewalls marked the dividing line without break —dividing them from what?

Surely the pillars were just on the other side of those draperies. Surely one more stride would carry them to the open air? Of course, it could not be otherwise.

He grasped the red cloth and tore it aside. Ahead of them was another vista, stretching away for many yards. Where, then, was the open door? Where the piazza? Where the free air?

He swung about in a dull rage, but the whisper his lips would have uttered remained, unformed in his throat for Tinker had vanished.

Blake held himself in hand. Here, he told himself sternly, was a problem that must be faced coolly. The first approach to panic would be his undoing and that of Tinker.

But what could have overtaken the lad?

He once more surveyed his surroundings with infinite care. He was certain that he had been heading straight enough for the door and the piazza. He knew he had got turned round even in the first confusion of finding those curtains clouding his path.

Then why hadn't he reached his objective?

His only answer was the blank stretch of red draperies, that mocked him by their sinister silence.

He examined the floor once more, but realised that this could tell him little. The hardwood blocks were set herring-bone fashion, thus slanting at an angle, either direction of which might lead towards or away from the door.

The long vista still stretched away in two directions, but the ends were still blocked by the same baffling red curtains. Upwards he could make out only a vague suggestion of what might be an arched roof.

He moved closer to the nearest side-curtains and, pressing his hand against the heavy cloth, pushed inwards, trying to discover if one of the pillars was on the other side.

The curtain yielded readily enough, but his hand encountered no obstruction. He repeated this experiment again and again as he moved along, but no sign of any pillar did he discover.

He knew that Tinker had not slipped behind one of the draperies in any attempt at a joke. The lad quite understood the seriousness of their business and had realised as well as Blake that things were developing along very sinister lines.

He was satisfied that something had reached out from the concealment of those maddening hangings and dragged the lad away —caught him with such swift precision as to make it impossible for him to cry out.

And this had happened in a flash while the lad had been standing within touching distance.

Blake closed his eyes and listened. He could hear not a sound. He would have called to Tinker, but he knew that any such effort would be a sheer waste of time. If the lad were able to make an effort he would soon let him (Blake) know.

With his eyes still shut, he reviewed every moment of the time since the first curtain had appeared in front of them. He checked every move he had made, every step. And the more he did so the more positive he was that when he had started to return to the door, he had been heading in the right direction.

But, then, how could that be unless the whole room had changed position? He had not swerved in his course. He had travelled too much in the dark; he had plodded too long through deep woods, not to be direction sensitive. He knew that it was utterly impossible that he had changed course in those few yards.

He opened his eyes and saw that the vista ahead of him no longer existed. He turned slowly and saw that the other way was also changed. Now, once more, he was standing within a small square room, eight feet or so each way, with only a faint light filtering from some invisible source to make him able to distinguish floor from those red curtains that seemed almost instantly to engulf what little light did reach the place.

And as he stood, silently and without any warning something else happened. He found himself covered by three automatics. They protruded through gaps in the curtain. Such was his surprise that, for a second or so, Blake stood rooted to the spot. Then as quietly as the guns had appeared they vanished. Blake stood again in the small space entirely surrounded by curtains. His first surprise over, Blake leapt towards the spot where one of the guns had poked through. Dragging the curtain aside, it was only to find another red drapery beyond.

He dragged another aside and, once more saw ahead of him, a sort of curtained corridor that stretched away some yards to a red end. Of the guns or the hands that held them, there was absolutely no sign, Blake began to follow the curtained corridor when suddenly on his left he found another such vista open invitingly. He could have sworn that his eyes had been on that very spot as he moved forward yet he had not seen the slightest movement to indicate that the curtains were being parted.

Should he follow it, he asked himself?

He made his decision quickly. It mattered not now into what he blundered. The sooner he reached a crisis of any kind, the better. It would bring him to actual handgrips with the power that had spirited away Tinker.

He changed his direction and strode on to the end. He dragged that drapery aside, to find as he anticipated, only another red wall a little farther on.

He did not go forward. Dropping the cloth he swung round to retrace his steps, but found the way he had come was closed.

But another vista was open, running from close to where he stood at a tangent to the way he had come. It was worse, far worse, far more confusing than any Hampton Court maze for that, at least, was built on an accepted mathematical formula which would yield to ordered analysis. It, whatever its problems, was based on solidity. This thing into which he had blundered was as fluid and unstable as water.

He was outwardly composed, but inwardly, he was seething with a deep anger.

He felt that all the time he was being watched, mocked, played with. He felt that in following each vista that opened, he was doing just what it was intended he should do. Yet he felt, too, that should he lose his self-control and dash madly at the nearest curtains, tearing them one after the other as quickly as possible, fighting recklessly, without reason to find a way through he would be doing what it was hoped he would do.

He walked on and, for the first time since he had got entangled in the whole maddening net, saw one of the fluted pillars just ahead of him. He approached it with quickened step. He would not confess to himself how eager he was to touch it, how much like an old friend it seemed. It stood there, mute, fluted but solid, something tangible in a world of red that was nothing.

He reached it. He laid his fingers on it and found pleasure in the contact with the cool marble. This, at least, was no mirage.

Standing beside the column, Blake closed his eyes once more and tried to remember the arrangement of the pillars. He recalled that, as he had stood on the threshold, an avenue had appeared to stretch directly ahead of him without any obstruction.

He recalled further, that the other 'avenues' visible from where he stood had run at a tangent from that —which meant that the columns were planted at regular intervals in an ordinary orthodox arrangement.

In that case, he told himself now, he should find another a few feet away —about eight if he remembered the distance correctly. Then it came to him that the size of the little 'rooms' formed by the curtains had been about this size, and he wondered if there was any connection between the two.

He opened his eyes and found the vista had not changed — neither forward nor back. Then he felt his way round the pillar, discovering himself in one of the little 'rooms' with which he was now becoming familiar.

Taking great care to mark the spot where this one pillar stood, he began to pace towards where he believed he should find another.

This brought him to a corner of the draperies where he probed against the curtains in every direction, but without finding what he sought.

He worked his way along patiently, extending his distance little by little until he knew he had covered a complete twelve foot radius of a full half circle, or in other words, a full twelve foot radius on that side of the pillar and vista from which he had started. Yet he found no sign of another column —only those same red, yielding draperies again and again and again.

He would not have been surprised if he failed now to return to the pillar that had been his base. But it stood just as he had left it.

As he pushed round it, however, he found himself in one of the same little rooms. The vista had again closed.

It didn't matter which way he went. He might remain where he was; or he might advance in the first direction that offered. Anything was better than standing still, he told himself.

So, aimlessly, he walked across the little room and dragged aside the curtain. He found a short corridor ahead of him which he followed. Just before he reached the end he saw another open space to the left.

He turned into this, and after covering half a dozen strides saw another corridor on his right. This carried him about a dozen paces before, at the end, he found another open space on the right.

And, as he swung round into this, he saw, not ten feet ahead of him, the open front door, the piazza and the free air beyond.

CHAPTER 12.   *Face to Face.*

DESPITE the self-control that was the achievement of many years, Sexton Blake stood in dumbfounded amazement at the vision before him. Common sense told him he had not blundered upon the way out any more than he had missed it before, because he had been confused in his sense of direction.

It was trickery. He knew that now just as he was dead certain he had reached this spot at a moment ordained by the same person who had played with him all this time.

Well, he would see what followed.

He walked steadily to the door and stepped out on to the veranda. His eyes went this way and that along the wide portico, and he had encountered too much since entering the place to find surprise in the sight of a white-clad man seated in the long cane chair reading as if he were entirely unaware that strangers had come to the island or the house.

Blake would have advanced upon him at once, but something urged him to turn and see if Tinker was to appear behind him. He did so, and all that had gone before was as nothing compared to the real shock he had in seeing that every vestige of the curtains was gone.

The vast, pillared interior was just as he had first seen it. Not a trace was there of those maddening, baffling draperies. They had vanished just as they had come.

Nor was there any sight of Tinker. That, at least, was no dream; though, for the other, Blake was asking himself if, after all, he would not wake to find himself lying on the beach —to realise that the whole thing was a vision of his unconsciousness.

Another thing, he quested in his mind. If it were not a dream, if it had actually happened, as he knew it had, then what motive lay behind it?

Was it in this manner all strangers were received who came to Mitkos? Was it thus that those others, who had, Blake had reason to believe, reached some central point in the mysterious organisation only to vanish, had been met?

Or were there definite suspicions against him? Was Tinker's disappearance a fluke, as it were, or had he deliberately been separated from him? The answer lie with that individual who lay stretched out in the chaise longue oblivious, apparently, of his presence.

In this moment, Sexton Blake knew that he would need to play his part well, if he were to get away with it.

How much did Goupolis know —that was the point. Yet the initiative lay with Blake and must be taken at once.

Remembering the role he was playing, remembering, too, that the man in the chair must know how he came ashore, and recalling the sinister maze he had just come through, he threw himself into his part with every ounce of dramatic art he possessed. His whole frame seemed to shrink. His shoulders were bowed submissively like those of a serf; his eyes became filled with an expression of humble pleading.

He held one hand in the other, "washing" them as if in great fear of the lord of the isle; he advanced, shufflingly, hesitatingly towards that immobile figure.

When he was within a couple of yards or so he paused, and his voice was thin, apparently terror-laden, as he quavered:

"Master."

Goupolis lowered his book and looked up.

"Well, then," he said in clipped, icy tones, speaking in modern Greek, "who are you, and what are you doing here?"

"Please do not be angry with me, lord. I am a poor Levantine sailor who has been shipwrecked."

"Why did you come up here? There was the village."

"The path led in this direction, lord. When we were thrown on the beach, master, we lay unconscious. When we awoke we came to seek aid. We ventured within and could find no one. Then I came out —to see you, lord. I have touched nothing, but I was long, for I became lost among the curtains."

"You say 'we'," snapped Goupolis. "What do you mean?"

"There was another, master —a youth. He has disappeared —lost among the curtains."

"Curtains —what, do you mean?"

"The curtains that hang within, master."

Goupolis waved towards the open door.

"There are no curtains there."

Blake turned his head and saw, through the open door, not a vestige of the red maze that had baffled him. He knew now that Goupolis was playing with him but, while Tinker was in unknown peril, he dared not change his course.

"I —I am confused, master," he stammered.

"You will have a chance to get your mind clear," responded Goupolis dryly.

At that moment he was at Blake's mercy. He was armed, but, before he could draw his gun Blake could reach him with his hands, could twist round that skinny neck upon his shoulders. And, had Blake realised what was to follow, he would have acted while the chance lay with him. But he waited, and, in doing so, placed himself utterly in the other's power.

"Yes, you will be taken care of," he heard Goupolis saying icily, "Whence came you?"

"From the south, lord."

"What port?"

"Myros."

"But that is close at hand. How came it you landed here? What were you doing at sea in the gale if Myros was your port?"

"We left port, lord, before the storm broke."

"And before that?"

"From Port Said."

"You travel far. But you will receive attention you should receive. I shall speak with you later. In the meantime, my servants will look after you. They have probably found your companion. That will do —for now."

And before he could speak, if he would, Blake felt himself grasped by powerful arms and, turning his head, found himself held by four stalwart, half-naked islanders.

It would be madness to resist now, he knew. There was menace enough in those last words he had heard, but he could not stave off that threat by precipitate action.

He knew now it was Goupolis; and he knew that Tinker had already been taken. His only course was to submit and watch for his chance. So he did not struggle. Instead, he bowed his head respectfully to Goupolis and allowed himself to be led away.

But, with him, he carried the vision of a swift, thin-lipped smile that dripped utter cruelty.

Blake was not greatly surprised when, on reaching the threshold of the big public room that led off the veranda, he found the whole interior once more, seemingly, obscured by a great red curtain.

Before his captors had time to guide him behind the nearest drapery he used his eyes calculating, trying to mark down some point as guidance. But he could see nothing beyond the red barricade, and when, just as he passed beneath the drawn folds, he turned his head to look back, he found that the way to the door was already lost.

When a second curtain had been lifted Blake saw, ahead of him, a vista such as had baffled him again and again when he and the lad had first got caught in the maze.

His captors, however, seemed to have no uncertainty about how they should go, for they proceeded straight ahead until they had covered what Blake made to be twenty paces. Then they turned sharp left, lifting the nearest side drapery to reveal a new vista.

This ended abruptly. But, to the right, appeared another short way, and then they drew aside curtain after curtain, the space between being only a few inches.

Followed a quick course to left, to right, along at an angle, straight ahead, more turnings, then another series of closer draperies, until, suddenly, Blake found himself standing in a narrow, dimly-lighted corridor.

He knew no more than when he and Tinker first essayed to find a way through the maze. He was quite positive that the confusion was not caused by the curtains alone. He believed there was some other factor concerned, but, so far, he could not fathom what it was.

In some way, though, they had come right through the great outer room into this corridor. He had seen no door; his captors had opened none to his knowledge, and he had used every observant faculty at top pressure.

He put the puzzle away in his mind for the time being, and concentrated on his present surroundings. The corridor might or might not be on the same level as the curtained room.

He had had no sensation of walking at any incline, either upwards or downwards. Yet he had seen so many mysterious things in the short time he had been in that house of curtains that he would not have been surprised at any revelation.

As a matter of fact, he was on a level very considerably lower than that of the room off the piazza. He was in the same corridor which Stefan Goupolis had followed on his way to the sea garden room, but farther along. He had come down during the period of time when he was passing through the curtains, but the whole puzzle was one to which an explanation was not to come until later.

As they moved along, Blake noticed they were travelling in a curve, at least, if he were to judge by the circular line of the nearest wall.

Then he discerned something liquid and smooth, like flowing ink or sable-dyed quicksilver. He peered at it closely. His captors seemed to have no objection.

He saw that it was a stream, and he realised that he must be underground, well below the surface.

They went past the door of the lift which Goupolis used, though Blake didn't know it. Then he saw the frosted stalactites, the clearer water beneath, the arched caves, and the narrow, black strand that had been hammered flat to a pathway.

Blake was more curious than ever to know what was in store for him. He had had more than one sample of the efficiency of the equipment in the villa and the power of Goupolis. But each moment his respect for the latter's power was growing deeper.

It would have been but first instinct had he put up a fight on the piazza when he was grabbed by the four who now held him. But he had resisted that impulse. To show his hand so plainly would have been, he believed, to vitiate all chance of any success.

He had come to Mitkos deliberately. He had passed through many dangers to arrive at that point in his investigations. He and Tinker had landed on a veritable wave of death. There was no going back now. And even were it not for those considerations he would have been forced to acquiesce in what was happening. That was the disappearance of Tinker.

He had to confess to himself, nevertheless, that it was difficult to see how he was to accomplish anything. Goupolis ruled as a petty monarch over all this island kingdom.

There was no doubt that he held power of life and death in his hands. If he chose to wreak that power on Blake and Tinker, who was to gainsay him?

Back in Port Said, Halloran had warned Blake he would find these conditions. Halloran had spoken too mildly. This island was one of the few places on the face of the globe where some recognised power would not or could not interfere.

Italy would leave it alone; Greece would fight shy; Turkey had other interests. Some day the question of national ownership would be settled. But Blake and Tinker might be lying dead a long time before that took place. And, whatever the result, no official inquiry would be made as to what had occurred during the rule of the overlord.

Yet Blake would not have left now even if he had seen a chance to do so. He felt that he had reached the end of his search.

He had as strong a hunch as had ever gripped him that he had come to the very centre of the web of the vast traffic which he was out to scotch.

In Marseilles, when he got the first actual location of the island, he had told himself that it would be an ideal point for transhipment of goods coming down from or going up to Constantinople and the Black Sea. It was more a cross-roads for that traffic as well as for east and west traffic of the Mediterranean than was Singapore for the Far East.

Moreover, it lay close to the mainland of Asia Minor. It was within easy reach of caravans passing from Tripolis on the coast across French Syria to Mosul, Turkey, the Caspian Republics. It was equally accessible for caravans leaving Beirut for Damascus and Haifa to cross Palestine to the Wahabi country and Iraq— every one of those routes being an inlet or outlet for the traffic.

The whole Maskelyne-like business he had already encountered was proof that the overlord was well prepared for unwelcome visitors. And it was easy enough to understand now how and why others who would have found the truth had never been heard of again.

But, even more important, was Tinker's fate.

Why had the lad been spirited away in such fashion? Why hadn't he (Blake) been selected? If Goupolis believed them to be what they professed to be —just two Levantine sailors —then why should Tinker have received such attention? It was this, more than anything else; that caused Blake to have an uneasy feeling that their real identity was suspected.

If that were so he would need every ounce of courage, subtlety, restraint and finesse that he could summon if they were to get out of the place alive.

He would not have been surprised had the whole of this chain of grottos through which he was now passing been suddenly obliterated by a falling of red curtains such as had baffled him above. But his captors kept straight on through the beautiful caves —caves that in themselves would have drawn travellers from afar —until suddenly they entered the sea-garden room with its domed glass sides and roof, its exquisite pearly light, its gorgeous, colourful marine garden beyond the thick plate windows.

If he had been stepping straight to his death, Sexton Blake would not have been able to repress the involuntary intake of breath at the exotic loveliness of the retreat. It was Vernesque in its conception and realisation, though even Jules Verne never imagined more perfection of detail. It was the creation of a genius; the playground of a multi-millionaire.

And then he saw Goupolis.

SEXTON BLAKE had no idea how Goupolis had reached the garden room.

But, having seen so much, he was not at all surprised that his host should be there to greet them; unless there were two of them exactly alike in appearance.

He was standing beside one of the fluted pillars close to the round glass view spot in the middle of the circular apartment, though what might be beneath that glass Blake couldn't guess —yet.

The same thin smile was playing about his lips as he watched his men lead Blake forward. It needed but a gesture for them to push Blake back against one of the pillars and secure him.

Goupolis, watching while he smoked an Egyptian cigarette that was packed with what Blake's nostrils told him was an exquisite blend, did not speak until the job was finished, and, at a wave of the hand, the four men had withdrawn,

"And now, Mr. Blake, we shall talk," he said softly in English.

Those words were all Blake needed to tell him that he might as well have come to the island heralded by trumpets; they were sufficient to fill him with an acute anxiety for Tinker.

He did not attempt to hedge. He knew it would be useless. How Goupolis had discovered the truth didn't matter now. The only thing that did matter was his and Tinker's escape. For he knew almost enough now to reward him for all he had gone through, and, if escape were possible, he would see to it that he took away enough evidence to bring into action forces strong enough to settle Goupolis for all time.

"It would surely have been as easy on the piazza," he rejoined coolly.

"So you are not foolish enough to carry the bluff farther," remarked Goupolis. "You are wise. You see, I have been expecting someone; but I wasn't sure that it was you until this very day. I have heard something of your blundering progress, my English friend."

"Quite interesting. Your spy service is good."

"You have had every proof."

"I do not deny that. But it won't serve you, Goupolis. The crust of your shell is breaking."

An extraordinary look of intense anger flamed for a moment in the eyes of the other; but it passed almost immediately, and his voice was still perfectly under control when he spoke.

"Crust of what, monsieur?"

"The word need not be spoken. You will know soon enough."

Goupolis laughed.

"I have heard of you, Monsieur Blake. I always gave you credit for possessing a little wit. But I find you are greatly overrated. Not only are you a blunderer, but you are stupid, a fool."

Blake shrugged as much as his bonds would permit.

"You are entitled to your opinion, Goupolis."

"You will find that I do not boast. I give you credit for bravery. You needed that to come here as you did. But that does not make you wise. You would have had wisdom to remain away. Others have tried to spy on Stefan Goupolis, and before he finished with them they have wished devoutly that they had not done so."

"The strength of your position is only apparent." remarked Blake lightly.

"What do you mean?"

Goupolis was squinting his eyes and leaning forward like a bird of prey. Blake knew the remark had got him going, as the saying is, and he did not intend to lessen the slight advantage it gave him. He only smiled.

"If you mean," said the other slowly, "that you have left word with someone in the outside world where you have come, it will serve you no more than if you had sent a message to the planet Mars. I am going to kill you. That is necessary. And I am going to kill the youth whom you rashly brought with you. That, too, is necessary. But before I do so I am going to give you such an experience, such a lesson, as you never anticipated. My only regret will be that some of your tribe will not be here to witness it. But I shall see that they learn the details."

"All right, get on with it," responded Blake carelessly.

"Are you going to tell me just why you came?"

"You mean am I going to tell you how much I know about you?"

"Have it that way if you prefer."

"Well, I am telling you nothing."

"Empty boast. You will sing a different tune before I finish."

He turned and gazed down through the thick plate glass into the deep tank where the giant squid was lurking. From this position against the pillar Blake could, by leaning outwards, also see a certain distance into the pit. But he soon found that Goupolis intended he should have a better view, for in some way that he could not perceive the pillar moved slowly and smoothly forward until it was at the very edge of the plate glass section. And now, unless he deliberately looked away, he found he could see right down to the white coral-like rocks and the snowy sand.

He heard Goupolis speaking again.

"It doesn't matter in the least now what you know about me or my island, monsieur. I am, in fact, rather pleased that you have come. Although I prefer my own company at most times there come moments when I find the need of a little relaxation. This is an occasion, and you will provide it."

"I am delighted."

"We shall see. At least you are of a different fibre from the last visitor. He, poor fool, was a clod, so I had to dispose of him quickly. But luckily we shall both enjoy the spectacle of how your young companion dies before I am left alone to watch you go the same way. We shall provide a pleasant little treat, and just so you may understand what I mean, I am going to give you a foretaste of what it means. I am sorry I cannot provide the spectacle of a human being before your companion furnishes the fun. Unfortunately I have no lawbreakers among my people at the moment. But a goat will serve as an illustration. So keep your gaze fixed on that view at your feet and you shall see."

If he had had the slightest notion of how Blake's heart had knotted within him while he spoke of Tinker he would certainly have prolonged the torture. For at first Blake had feared that the lad was to be sent to his death in some fiendish way before his very eyes, while he stood helpless to lift a finger to save him.

But a goat as an illustration. His heart seemed to turn over a dozen times in the utter relief that swept over him. What he would be able to do when the actual moment did come he could not see. But every moment's delay was precious.

His face, however, was perfectly impassive as he continued to gaze down into the pit while Goupolis approached another of the pillars and pressed it at a certain spot. Then he turned back to the edge of the plate glass, and so intent was the expression in his eyes that Blake perforce had to gaze downwards, too.

He had not long to wait. He heard Goupolis tap, tap, tapping on the glass with his foot. He saw one long, purplish-black tentacle emerge from the rocky lair, saw the second repulsive sucker end move into the open, then glimpsed the horrible thing to which they were joined.

He knew now what it was. He had seen the giant squid in the West Indies, but he had never expected to see such a monster here on an island in the eastern Mediterranean.

He watched coolly, critically, while the creature came forth more and more, recognising that tap, tap, tapping above as the invariable prelude to a living tit-bit that it could becloud with its vile liquid and engulf within its repulsive maw.

Up and up through the crystal clear water the twin tentacles rose, the sucker lips at the ends showing plainly now as they opened and closed to "sense" the anticipated treat.

Blake could not distinguish any means of delivering food to the horrible monster, and as the feelers groped at the very surface of the plate glass just beneath where he stood he wondered if there was some secret trap by which he would be precipitated into that horrible, gaping, purplish orifice.

The thought sent a chill up and down his spine. He recoiled against the pillar but recovered immediately. He knew if Goupolis had seen his action he was quite capable of using it as a means of further amusing himself.

Then it happened.

From somewhere almost immediately beneath his feet something shot into view. There was a wild disturbance of the water as the squid's tentacles sought for its prize. Blake had just time to discern the white, hairy body of a goat, had one brief glimpse of the poor creature's terrified eyes, before a vile cloud of purplish fluid swept throughout the water, beclouding it, saturating it so that only the churning surface told what a ghastly thing was happening beneath.

"And so you see, my English friend, how it is done."

He turned his head as Goupolis spoke. He saw the Greek gazing at him with an ironic smile. And he knew then that Goupolis was completely without mercy, for the light of eager blood-lust was in his eyes.

The man might be the cunning and powerful head of the great international drug conspiracy; he might be multimillionaire and overlord of the Isle of Mitkos. But he was mad. Of that Sexton Blake was certain.

And he would prefer to deal with a dozen desperate criminals who were sane than with one who was insane. A chill of real fear pervaded Blake as this realisation struck him.

He knew that the slightest hint that he was feeling the effects of the ghastly scene he had just witnessed might be the spur to send Goupolis ahead to finish the whole thing in one evening's orgy. He knew by what a slender thread hung his chance of getting in touch with Tinker before the lad and he went to satisfy the cravings of the monster in the pit.

He reproached himself bitterly for bringing Tinker with him. He told himself now in this situation of such desperate need that he should have insisted on the lad leaving him at Port Said.

But there was no use in repining now. The die was cast. And it was plain enough that Goupolis had passed sentence on both of them without any other trial than his own determination to wipe out utterly all persons who dared to approach his secret.

"Perhaps when you see your young friend you will be inclined to tell me the few things I wish to know." Goupolis was saying while Blake thought so desperately. "We shall continue our entertainment later in the evening. I am waiting for further news through the ether regarding you, monsieur. I have sent out an inquiry to discover some things which my own organisation will be able to answer. You will have an opportunity to ponder on the mutability of things until I am ready. But first we shall see what a search of your person will reveal."

He clapped his hands lightly as he spoke, and, immediately, the four men who had withdrawn appeared.

Up to now Blake had been congratulating himself that Goupolis had made no suggestion of a search. Not that anything could be revealed by this unless it were prosecuted with a thoroughness that would be very exceptional.

But there was, nevertheless, a secret about his somewhat sparse personal equipment which, now, more than ever, he was anxious to conceal. For upon it depended, he knew, the only hope of life for him and Tinker.

Before leaving London Blake had considered the question with the greatest care. He knew that, in going upon this mission, he could not depend upon the ordinary means of supplying himself with funds.

So absolutely necessary was it that he should not, in the very slightest way, become connected with anything touching officialdom that he had decided he must carry upon his person sufficient money to see him through for a certain period of time. If he ran short before he had achieved his purpose, then he must depend on his wits to supplement his needs.

Thus, when he and Tinker left London, they were travelling light, both as regards luggage and money documents. In fact, they took for clothing only what they wore; not even a toothbrush did they add. Those little articles necessary to personal hygiene were things that they must depend on securing as the need arose.

For money, Blake provided two body belts. And it was while he was planning the exact arrangement of these that he hit on his big plan. It remained to be seen whether this, on which he had been counting as his chief asset in a tight corner, should be snatched from his grasp.

But he knew that the slightest sign of anxiety would bring about the very thing he was trying to avoid. So he still kept his air of cool indifference.

"Your search will reveal nothing of interest," he drawled. "But I am entirely at your service, monsieur."

"Whether you wish, or no," jeered Goupolis.

He took out a small but efficient-looking automatic pistol and held it in readiness. Then he addressed his men in Greek.

"Strip the prisoner to the skin," he ordered.

Blake submitted without a struggle. No matter what means of attack or defence he might possess he could do nothing effective against that weapon that was trained on his heart. Common sense told him he must either wait for or make a chance later.

As a matter of fact he got no chance in any event. Those four Greeks of the islands knew their business.

While two of them loosened the bonds that secured Blake's torso to the pillar, the other pair drew off the loose jersey he had been wearing, the under waistcoat and a rough woollen vest.

Each garment, under Goupolis' keen eye was gone through as carefully as if Blake were being shipped to Devil's Island. Seams, linings, pockets, even buttons and collarband were given a minute inspection.

Then the waistcoat received the same attention, and, finally, the vest. But not even a grain of a suspicious nature rewarded their attention.

The ropes were drawn taut again, and those that secured his lower limbs were loosened. It was now that the body belt was revealed, and, at sight of the metal studded, broad band of leather, the eyes of the Greek lit with anticipation.

"Off with it, off with it," he cried. "Secure him again and give it to me."

He smiled thinly at Blake, but the latter could see a very watchful look in his eyes. And it needed all Blake's powers of self-control to stand unchanging of expression beneath those probing eyes for he knew that now was to come the real test.

He held his air of indifference while the follows obeyed their master. But not until the lower ropes were hauled taut and secured again did Goupolis put away his automatic.

Then he picked up the belt, and, from beneath suddenly lowered lids, Blake watched him while he ran his fingers along the inside, found the flaps of the different pockets, and, opening them, allowed the contents to fall into his hand.

There seemed little to reward him.

There was an oilskin packet which he unfolded with unconcealed eagerness only to emit a curse when he found it packed with a bit of tobacco and a packet of cigarette papers.

He cursed again when a double-ended cartridge proved to contain nothing but matches —the latter, and the tobacco and paper as dry as could be despite Blake's immersion in the water.

There were some gold coins, Greek and Italian, to the value of about twenty pounds in all. There was, too, a bunch of Egyptian piastre notes still sodden from the water.

Finally, there was another oilskin packet which Goupolis found contained only a miniature pad of writing paper and a little leather case containing a tiny propelling pencil and fountain pen.

He lifted his head sharply to find Blake smiling at him.

"I hope you are satisfied, monsieur," Blake remarked lightly, "I told you you would get little for your pains. My poor effects can be of little value to one of your wide possessions. Still —if the gold is acceptable —"

Goupolis landed close in front of Blake in two powerful springs. It looked as if he would bring his hand across Blake's mouth, and

Blake braced himself for the shock of the blow. But, with an effort, the Greek controlled himself.

"Enough." he hissed. "Were it not that I have much in store for you I would slay you as you stand. But I will wait —for my pleasure."

With the belt dangling in his hand he swung round to his men, who, evidently knowing what danger lay in the overlord's anger, were cowering together.

"Strip him," he snapped. "Make haste."

They obeyed, loosening the leg ropes once more so that Blake's nether garments could be dragged from him. But though these were subjected to the same careful scrutiny that had been given to his other garments, they yielded nothing.

"Why don't you try the wrecked pattimar," asked Blake quietly. "You might find something there."

Goupolis ignored the jibe.

"Put those things on again," he ordered.

Blake submitted far more readily than the Greek could guess. He was, in truth, on tenterhooks, lest he should not have his belt returned to him. But when, at last, Goupolis tossed it to one of his men, Blake heaved an inward sigh of terrific relief, though, for reasons of his own, he was in a fever of alarm as he watched one of the fellows fumbling clumsily at the long, heavy metal buckle.

For, therein, lay Sexton Blake's secret.

CHAPTER 14. The Glass Chute.

BLAKE never knew what hour it was when he was hauled out of his cell later that evening.

Following the search in the marine room he had been led back along the path than led through the grottos and pushed into a narrow cell.

He had been left unbound, and by the time he had finished a tour of his pitch dark quarters he realised that Goupolis knew he had nothing to fear that he would make his escape.

The door was of heavy steel. He had seen that when it was opened for him to be pushed through. But floor and walls were of solid stone, and, though he leaped upwards again and again, he could discover no signs of any window.

It was only later, when his eyes became more accustomed to the blackness, that he was able to distinguish, faintly, a barren patch of starlight sky overhead.

This meant, he told himself, that air and light came through that small barred grating, though how high above his head it was or whether it was on ground level he could not tell. All his efforts to reach it failed.

There was not even a wooden bench to sit upon; no chair, no table. The place was more barren than a rat hole, for that might have contained a few wisps of straw.

Blake squatted on the cold stone and pondered on his position. Try as he would he could not shake off the fearful depression that assailed him.

He had been hoping more than he had realised that he would have been given at least a sight of Tinker so that he could send the lad a signal of hope.

But Goupolis had seemed to close up like an oyster after his failure to find anything in the body-belt; or, at any rate, after Blake had openly jeered at him.

Blake knew, however, that the devil intended some ghastly form of retaliation, and, after seeing the fate of the poor goat, it was not difficult to guess what form it would take.

Nor was the Greek forgetting to let him know that he would introduce the refinement of torture. He said he knew something of Sexton Blake. That was probable and so he would know, too, just what Tinker meant to Blake. He would know that Blake was like a father to the lad as well as a comrade. The whole world knew that. And that knowledge would be enough for him to surmise pretty well what Blake would suffer if he were forced to stand by and watch the lad go to a horrible death.

He hunched his knees and groaned aloud. In sheer desperation he felt that he would tear at the solid walls in order to reach the lad. Yet he knew that would only be a futile exhibition in which Goupolis would revel.

There was no telling but what the Greeks were posted somewhere close at hand even now, watching and waiting to witness his suffering. He must not give in to panic. He would need every ounce of his wit to get himself and the lad out of this impasse.

Yet, rack his brain though he would, he could not see anything ahead but inevitable doom.

What could he do? What power could he employ? Goupolis was surrounded with man power and mechanical power. He was lord of the isle and subject to none. In his hands, on Mitkos, was power of life and death. If he chose to employ torture who was to say him nay?

None.

There was no other answer. Nor did Blake find one through the time that dragged like an eternity. He possessed only one thing that might prove in any way effective. But that would serve nothing unless a chance could be made to employ it.

Nevertheless he would leave no straw untested. And, to that end, he bent down and began to unlace his heavy boots. He drew the long laces out, one at a time, and, measuring a half by the simple method of doubling it, he began to saw at the point of bend against the rough nails on the heel of his boot.

When the lace was cut through he laid one half aside and began to relace the other. It did not reach the top as before, but it came high enough for him to secure the boots so that his trousers would fall over them when he stood up. He knew that, did the gap show beneath, Goupolis would spot it quickly enough.

He attached the lace of the second boot in the same manner. When the job was finished he took one length, and, getting his hands up beneath his body belt, made a loop round one of the straps over the hip.

He let that dangle until he had looped the second bit of lace round the strap on the other hip and then he brought the two ends together in the small of his back, keeping them under the body belt so that it should cover them.

Holding them thus he stood up and drew them tight. When he felt the two hip straps drawn taut, he tied the loose ends firmly so that when he loosened the belt, his trousers hung snugly enough on his hips.

He tested the body belt at three different holes before he was satisfied with its hang. The test consisted of his pulling his heels together and his thigh muscles taut so that, by a quick squirming of his body, the belt slid to the floor, yet, when his limbs and muscles were natural, it hung in place.

There was no more he could do. Squatting back on the floor he gave himself up to thoughts as unenviable as can find lodgement in a man's mind; for he held himself responsible for what might be Tinker's fate.

Thus he still sat when they hauled him out.

He did not resist. Now that the moment of test had come he was eager enough to face it.

He was taken along once more to the marine-room, where he found Goupolis sitting smoking.

He had changed into a dinner jacket, and, from this fact as well as that his smoke was a cigar, Blake deduced that he had both dined and slepped.

Goupolis left him in no doubt on that score. In fact, now that he was closer, Blake saw on the smoking table beside the chair, a bunch of grapes, a cup of coffee and a little clock that showed it was two o'clock in the morning.

The Greek seemed to have recovered his equanimity of temper, for he smiled as he said pleasantly:

"I trust you will not think me remiss in my duties as a host, but really, I saw no reason why you should dine considering that you will need no material sustenance where you are going."

Blake matched his smile.

"It would be a pity to waste anything, Goupolis, but I have always understood that even a condemned man is permitted what he desires just before his doom —a drink or a cigarette, at least."

"You shall have them," jeered the Greek. "But not yet. I am going to show you something."

He rose and laid the remnant of his cigar in a tray. Then he made a curt gesture to the four men who held Blake and led the way past the plate-glass top of the pit of horror to the door which led to his wireless control-room.

He opened the door and stepped just inside as the powerful lights came on. Blake was pushed to the threshold where he could see all the gleaming instruments and keys and vulcanite gadgets.

He wondered why Goupolis should bother to deliver an address on the various instruments, their use and so on, until he realised that the man was a genuine fanatic about such things.

Nor could he see how this private knowledge which the other was importing could ever be of use to him. But because Sexton Blake would never give in entirely to despair until Death should have him finally, he listened with almost flattering attention, absorbing every word, and when the other paused, saying with an enthusiasm that really impressed Goupolis:

"I congratulate you. Under other conditions I should certainly have enjoyed to witness a demonstration of the various instruments. I have seen other control-rooms, but never anything finer."

Goupolis looked at him almost friendlily.

"What a pity, what a pity," he murmured. "But it is a greater pity that I cannot show you more. I have a hangar a short distance from the house that holds two fast and powerful aeroplanes, one a small personal machine, the other a long-distance cruiser. And my submarine —it is a great pity you cannot see it. You will have noticed my large yacht in the harbour?"

Blake inclined his head in assent.

"There is nothing finer afloat. And I have other craft as well. You will begin to realise, my English friend, what a fool you were to make such a rash attempt as to seek out Stefan Goupolis. I am immune from the greatest powers on earth. What did you, alone, expect to accomplish?"

"I am not dead yet, Goupolis."

If Blake had desired deliberately to precipitate matters he could have said nothing more warranted to achieve his purpose. All the man's geniality left him in a flash. He weaved to the men to drag Blake back. He was cursing in a low tone as he came out and closed the door. Then he stood for a moment eyeing Blake.

"I was almost forgetting," he snarled. "The best of the

entertainment is yet to come. We shall lose no more time."

He walked along a little way and opened another door. He disappeared from view but Blake was pushed after him quickly, and now he saw that he was in a sort of narrow passage that ran along the side of a narrow, glass-paved strip in the floor.

At this moment the place broke into brilliant illumination, a glare even appearing beneath the glass strip which Blake could estimate now as being about two feet across.

At first he was puzzled to know what it could be. It was a boxed-in chute, all glass it seemed and running at a sharp slope. He looked farther along to where Goupolis was standing and found the Greek smiling at him with that same, thin-lipped, cruel smile he had begun to hate violently.

Goupolis motioned for the fellows to bring Blake along, and, as he went forward, Blake saw, suddenly, the whole beastly horror of the thing

For, lying bound on a flat shelf at the end of the chute was Tinker.

The sight drove Blake to a frenzy. His muscles stiffened involuntarily in the terrific effort he made to control himself. His captors must have been warned, for they tightened their hold. Goupolis was grinning.

But Blake did not see him. His eyes had sought Tinkers. The lad was gazing back at him, full-eyed, courageously, his lips parted in a smile.

In those few moments they spoke to each other as fully as though they used real words, so deep was their understanding each of the other.

But the situation looked even more desperate than Blake had feared. He knew now the meaning of that sloping chute. He knew that the moment Tinker was pushed or rolled off the narrow platform on which he lay he would slide down the chute at an ever-increasing speed until he plunged into the jaw of that filthy, repulsive Thing that lay in wait. This was how the goat had gone.

He turned to Goupolis, who was watching him.

"It seems to be your trick, Goupolis," he said, finding it difficult to keep his voice level. "Is there anything I can offer to save his life? I cannot give my own, for it is already in your power. But there might be things I could tell you —things you might find it worth while to

104

know."

It was as bold a gesture as, in his helplessness, he could make. Nor did he expect anything from it. He was fighting for time. He would use any means to gain that precious thing.

His brain seemed to have stopped functioning. It seemed that this terrible crime could not take place —that something must happen to stop it. Yet he knew that it needed but one touch to send Tinker sliding to that horrible death.

He had relaxed. He wanted to know that he had some chance of breaking free when the last critical moment should come.

He was watching Goupolis so closely that he almost betrayed himself. But the Greek was engrossed in thought. Blake's words had caused him to wonder if it were worth while getting out of this poor English fool some information about how he had come to take up the hunt.

He might have begun to ask questions were it not that the one tiny chance that Blake had been waiting for came, it was no more than a slight lessening of the pressure on his arms and body due to the four who held him watching Goupolis closely to know his will.

Blake seized it, casting everything into that one final desperate throw. He had already stiffened his thighs, so that the body-belt was slipping over his legs. Now he drew his feet tight together, felt the belt slither down past his knees, then he broke into a perfect human fury.

CHAPTER 15. *The Secret of the Belt*

SEXTON BLAKE did not attempt to overpower his four gaolers.

He knew that, long before he could accomplish that, Goupolis would have out his automatic and drill him. His aim was to break free, and, so furious was the surprising effort he made, that he did break away before the four had a chance to recover.

Blake dived to the floor and grabbed the body-belt. Then, even while Goupolis, cursing at his men, was clawing at his automatic, Blake reached him.

Goupolis must have seen the heavy belt in his hand, and concluded that Blake intended using the buckle as a beater. But Blake made no attempt to do so. Instead, he grabbed Goupolis by the neck with his left hand, and, with his right, pressed the now freed tongue of the belt against the flesh.

During these few hectic moments his fingers had been busy with the long metal frame of the buckle, and as the point of the tongue pressed the flesh something shot out from it like the tip of a needle, puncturing to the depth of a quarter of an inch or so.

Had one been able to see how Blake's fingers were employed they would have seen that the pressure was bringing the two parallel sides of the buckle closer and closer, for it was nothing more or less than a very cunningly contrived hypodermic syringe which he had filled in London with a powerful narcotic drug that would act within a few seconds. It was when he realised that he would be unable to carry a gun on him when he reached the final point of his mission, when he knew that, if he were captured, he would probably be subjected to a very close search, and all personal belongings taken from him except those that appeared harmless and essential to the primitive form of dress, that the idea had come to him.

And that was why he had been on tenterhooks until it was given back to him.

So swiftly had he acted, so instantaneous was the action of the drug, that Goupolis was sagging in his arms before the other four could reach him.

Blake used no gentleness with Goupolis. He held him as a shield in front of him until he managed to get hold of the automatic; then he let him flop to the floor in a heap while he jerked up the weapon and pulled the trigger.

The foremost fellow went down even while Blake fired the second shot. The one who had been close behind whirled round as if an invisible hand had gripped him, stumbled, recovered, then came on again.

Blake had swung the pistol to a different angle and sent two more quick shots, each of which found a billet. One man crashed to the floor, but the other took the lead with scarcely a pause, and plunged forward, a knife in his hand.

Blake fired again. This time the fellow was stopped for a moment, but then he recovered, and when Blake dragged on the trigger again he got nothing but a dead click.

He leaped over the prostrate body of Goupolis and drove the pistol into the face of the nearest man. It steadied him back, blood streaming from the deep gash the metal had made.

Blake was just in time to meet the determined rush of his fellow, and, despite the use of the weapon as a club, the knife ripped down the side of his arm.

Blake hammered with the pistol again. The fellow still lurched towards him driving him back. By this time the other had recovered, and, though blinded by blood, threw his great arms about Blake.

Blake braced against him, concentrating on the other, who seemed as if he must be made of iron. He knew that this was the one he must "out" if he were to win.

He used every atom of remaining strength in the next blow, and this time the islander went down to stay.

But now, as he gave his attention to the remaining fellow, a cold chill ran down Blake's spine as he realised he was being dragged on to the glass top that covered the chute. If he were hurled down on to that surface, if he went through on to the slope, nothing could save him.

He stiffened, and then yielded a little. The other was struggling quite blindly, knowing only what he had to do, and determined to do it. Blake sensed that he, too, was thinking about the chute, and was doing his best to send Blake crashing into it.

Blake put every ounce of strength he could muster into that last effort. He felt his foot slither on to the smooth glass, and knew that he was on the verge of the death that Goupolis had planned for him.

He dragged his foot back, only to feel the other slide on to the glass. It was like crawling along a slippery treadmill or trying to climb an icy slope. And, all the time, the wounded, crazed fellow who to the end would do his duty to the master he feared was pushing him back.

Blake got both feet off the glass for a moment and fought to make headway. But the other, with a giant effort, threw him back once more, until Blake knew both feet were well on the brittle surface.

In a second or so he would be through. What could he do? Tinker was bound and helpless. If he —Blake —were overpowered the lad would quickly suffer a like fate. He must do something to offset the purpose of this devil who held him. But what?

His foot slid again, and then, all of a sudden, he gave up entirely any resistance. The result was instantaneous. The terrific strength which the other had been exerting sent Blake slithering right across the glass top of the chute until his legs followed on to the solid floor beyond, leaving only the upper part of his body to fall on the glass.

Blake heard a terrific smashing sound; then all he knew was that he was clawing at anything to save himself while the other had fallen away from him.

He was safe on solid floor before he realised what had happened. The other had gone to the fate intended for him.

Blake staggered to his feet. His head was reeling, and he realised that he was trembling violently. The strain and action he had endured without food for many hours was telling on him.

But he knew that every moment was precious. Goupolis was out of the game for many hours to come —at least forty if there had been no leakage of the quantity of the drug he had stored in the buckle syringe.

One of his men was gone to a fate that filled Blake with nausea to think of. The other three would be good for nothing even if they survived. He had neither the strength nor the time to give them any attention now. It was Tinker and himself. Self-survival is, after all, the first fundamental law of nature. And Tinker must be rescued before others came.

He got down on to his knees and peered through the glass to where the lad was lying, his eyes eloquent with the feelings roused in him by the terrible battle he had witnessed.

Just in front of Blake was the jagged edge of the break caused by the crash of his vanished opponent. He found that, by sitting down and using the heavy heel of his boot, he could break the brittle material bit by bit so that it would drop into the chute and slide away.

He worked quickly, but with care that none of the loose bits should reach the unprotected lad. Then, with an effort that sapped his remaining strength, he managed to get hold of Tinker, and, little by little, get him up over the side.

Once he had him on the floor there was no difficulty in loosening his bonds. And, as soon as Tinker felt himself free, he scrambled to his feet, stammering clumsily what he felt.

Blake cut him short with a gesture.

"We've got to get out of here, young 'un. There is no telling how soon the gang at the village will be here. Also we don't know how many there are in the house. We haven't found any cache of drugs, but I've had enough admissions out of Goupolis to put him away for the rest of his life."

"Will you leave him here, guv'nor?"

"Nothing else to do. He won't stir for forty hours or more."

"What about the others?"

"Can't attend to them now. I've got a plan. If we can get away we may be able to bring it off."

"I'm ready, guv'nor. What do you wish me to do?"

"Unless Goupolis was lying there is a hangar near the house with a couple of 'planes standing in it. The risk of trying to get away by boat is too great. But we may be able to manage by 'plane if we can get a clear run. It all depends on whether the machine is ready for immediate work, and, knowing Goupolis as I now do, I fancy he will have everything primed for a quick getaway at any time. We've got to find that hangar without loss of time. Come on."

He retreated along the passage until he came to the door leading to the marine-room. When they were through, Blake made a quick study of the lock until he solved the secret of how the spring was worked from the marine-room side. Then he slammed it shut, leaving the four men lying inside.

"They've just got to stay there until we get back —if ever," he grunted.

"How are we coming back, guv'nor?"

"I'm going to find some official power. We've got the whole League of Nations behind us, and I know enough now to smash the very heart of this conspiracy. I'm going to try the Island of Rhodes if we get away. But the first thing is to find our way up to ground level.

If we get mazed up in more of those curtains we are done for."

He led the way back through the grottos, making use of the bits of knowledge he had gained by close scrutiny during his previous journeys. He had only a distant glance for the circular glass top of the pit. He had no desire to gaze into those depths now. He knew only too well what foulness that beclouded horror would suggest.

It was Tinker who found the grill that opened into the small lift. As soon as he understood what it meant Blake realised that here they probably had the key to escape.

It took considerable time to learn the secret of the release catch, but by a systematic covering of the wall on each side, and working on the same theory as that of the other door through which they had come, they succeeded.

The actual mechanism was quite orthodox. Entering, they closed the door, realising as they did so the danger of being imprisoned were they to fail to get out elsewhere. But that was a risk that had to be taken, and each heaved a sigh of relief as the lift shot upwards in response to Blake's pressure on the upper of two buttons.

The door that faced them when they came to a stop opened quite easily. They stepped into a corridor, and then, exploring, found a door that opened into the big pillared room off the piazza.

There were no curtains to confuse them, but, remembering their former experiences, Blake advanced with the utmost caution. Only two lights were burning in the place, the upper part being lost in deep shadows. But another light on the piazza showed the outline of the main doorway, and, after measuring the distance carefully, Blake reached a hand back to Tinker.

"We'll run it, young 'un," he whispered.

"Ready —go!"

They sprinted at top speed through the aisles of columns, expecting each moment to find themselves brought up by a tangle of draperies. Nothing happened, and only Blake himself knew how deep was his breath of relief when they stood safely on the piazza.

But that was only a step on the road to escape. They had yet to find the hangar, to avoid discovery by any guards who might have been placed, to get one of the 'planes into flight and to soar into the night sky over the unknown (to them) waters.

They reached the ground and faded into the shadows. Blake led the way down the terraces, until they found a path leading to the right.

Earlier on he had noticed that the land off that way seemed to be more flat than elsewhere, and now, as he considered, he told himself that it would be the spot he would choose were he to build a hangar and take-off ground.

Ten minutes of scrambling through bushes, over rough ground and along a shallow ditch, brought them all of a sudden to the edge of what seemed to be a wide, sloping platform.

Further investigation showed it to be the roof of a building almost flush with the ground, and when they had worked round one corner they found a vast, open well of darkness in front of them.

Although Blake's body-belt had been stripped of its contents, Tinker had been left in possession of the few simple items which the pockets of his had contained. It was a strange place for him to bring into use the matches which had been so carefully stored, and little had either he or Blake guessed that one of them was to come into play at a vital moment on the island of Mitkos in the Aegean Sea.

Its tiny flame guided them to a switch on the wall. Blake had his hand on the lever by the time the flame flickered out. Then, with his free hand, he drew Tinker close.

"I don't know what this will do. But be ready. If Goupolis told the truth, and there are two machines here, pick the smaller. I'll be close after you."

He felt Tinker tense himself for a quick dash, then he dragged down on the switch lever.

It was as if a magic hand had swung a miniature sun into the place. The whole interior was studded with bulbs which sprang info brilliant illumination as the connection was made.

Flinging round Blake saw Tinker racing towards the smaller of two graceful aeroplanes which stood as if ready to spring forward of their own volition.

He had time to notice that they were standing in a perfectly designed underground hangar with a gradual slope running to the ground for the take-off. That was all, before he followed the lad.

He heard Tinker utter an exclamation as he climbed into the cockpit. He jerked a question. The lad sent back a quick answer. Then Blake sprang for the propeller. That quick give and take of words had told him all he wanted to know. It was a standard Comet three-seater of British make —a machine which Tinker understood perfectly and had flown several times. It was, to the lad, like taking the wheel of the

Grey Panther.

And, as the engine roared out, both he and Blake knew that the die was cast.

Blake climbed in after Tinker. The lad waggled the joy-stick and the machine started forward. They went up the incline smoothly and gently, reached flat, open ground beyond; then, as they gathered more and more speed, Tinker put her to the rise, alarmed at a dimly-seen bulk of trees ahead.

The little machine took the air like a bird. Tinker circled, getting the feel of things while Blake peered at the few scattered lights which marked the village with one brilliant one that he knew must be at the top of the wireless tower. Then Tinker straightened out and headed out to sea.

In another hour dawn would begin to unfold.

CHAPTER 16.   The End of Goupolis.

THE sun was just clearing the coastal Hills of the island of Rhodes, that classic isle which loomed so large in ancient history and which is now the largest of the Italian Dodecanese group of Asia Minor, when Commander Guilio Torrini, of the Italian light cruiser Roma, gazed from the bay of his bridge to see what at first appeared to be a large bird in the sky.

But his experienced eyes soon discerned it to be an aeroplane that was coming towards the ship in an almost direct line. Commander Torrini called the attention of the officer on duty to the sight, and both had surmises to pass as to whence it had possibly come and whither it might be bound, agreeing that it was most likely one of the frequent long-distance flights nowadays so popular.

It seemed to be flying quite smoothly, and the watchers were a good deal surprised, therefore, when it dipped suddenly, circled and dropped at a steep angle towards the water.

They could see plainly enough that it was not a seaplane, so their amazement was the greater when the machine, still going quite smoothly, flattened out a few feet above the water, then, deliberately on the part of the pilot it seemed, took the smooth surface with a splash. The men on the bridge of the cruiser were still more amazed when they saw two figures crawl along one of the wings, stand up, wave frantically, then deliberately dive into the sea while the 'plane began to settle.

Within a few minutes the cruiser had been brought dead astern, a motor-boat was dashing towards the swimming figures, and within another twenty minutes two bedraggled, disreputable-looking persons were standing before Commander Torrini.

He listened to the story which the taller of the two had to tell. The relation was given in fluent Italian, but when the commander spoke it was in excellent English.

"So you say you are Mr. Sexton Blake," he remarked. "It may be so. I have heard much of that gentleman. I know England very well. I was naval attache at the Italian Embassy for some time. But it will be a comparatively simple matter to prove your words. If you are indeed that gentleman we shall be happy to extend our full hospitality to you. It is odd, nevertheless, that you should arrive upon the sea close to us at this particular time."

"May I ask why?" ventured Blake, also using English.

"Because I am on my way to hoist the Italian flag on the island of Mitkos. The dispute between Greece and Italy regarding the island has been settled to the advantage of my country. But I cannot go into further details until I corroborate your story. If what you say is the truth —well, we shall soon clean out that nest."

"I only beg you to make wireless inquiries as soon as possible," rejoined Blake. "If you go to establish Italian sovereignty on Mitkos, you will have the exact authority needed to deal with Goupolis. Might I suggest that you put one inquiry through to Scotland Yard, in London, addressed to Inspector Thomas? He will be able to confirm that I and my assistant left London some weeks ago on a secret mission. If you will insert the single code word, 'Annihilate,' he will know that I am the one concerned. It should be sufficient proof."

Commander Torrini smiled as if he were beginning to believe that this amazing and almost incredible story really had some truth in it.

"At any rate," he said informally and with kindness, "you will both want to bath and change. We shall provide you with some clothes; then, I think, breakfast is indicated."

By the time Blake and Tinker emerged from the privacy of the quarters that had been allotted to them they presented a startling contrast to the two ragged-looking Levantines who had been picked up in the water. With most of the stain scrubbed off, in clean white uniforms and piped shoes, they gave, in their appearance, more confirmation of the story they had told than anything else.

But other confirmation had come as well. They found Commander Torrini waiting for them. His eyes widened as he saw them; then he put out his hand, smiling.

"It is indeed you, Mr. Blake," he said genially. "I have received a prompt wireless from your New Scotland Yard. The code word has been answered with another. As a matter of form I will ask you to give it to me."

"'Spider'," answered Blake promptly.

"Quite correct. Now let us go to breakfast. There is a great deal I would have you tell me. Then we shall decide just what steps we shall take when we reach Mitkos."

"What time do you expect to reach there, commander?"

"We are doing about twenty-two knots. We shall be there, at that rate, about two o'clock this afternoon."

"In that event, I hope we shall find Goupolis as we left him."

It was just past one o'clock that afternoon when the smudge that was Mitkos appeared ahead. Blake had warned Commander Torrini about the steel bars that guarded the entrance to the harbour. Torrini had assured him that he would not risk his ship in any event without a local pilot to take them through.

The cruiser thundered out one warning shot, then the launch was lowered away and, with Blake acting as pilot, edged in through the twin heads, her boatload of sailors out of sight in the cabin.

As they nosed the beach they were met by half a dozen men, one of whom announced himself as the wireless operator. Explanations were brief enough. He submitted without a struggle, and, in reply to the commander's questions, stated that he knew nothing of the whereabouts of his master, Signor Goupolis, but he believed he had left in the night in his private aeroplane.

This sounded to Blake and Tinker as if nothing was known, even yet, of what had happened in the villa the night before, and when he suggested to Torrini that no time should be lost in investigating matters at the villa, the latter agreed with him.

Blake took the lead now. The handful of islanders were left on the beach under the guard, but the rest, under the personal command of Torrini followed Blake and Tinker up the path to the piazza.

Blake was wary again as he stepped into the pillared room, but the mechanism was still out of play, for no curtains obstructed their passage. They descended in the small lift, three at a time, but when the second load had reached the bottom they went ahead through the grottos to the marine-room.

Blake went straight to the door leading to the place where he had had his terrible fight. He had told the commander the details of that battle, and, as he pressed the secret spring and opened the door, the first thing that met their gaze was proof of what he had said.

Three men, wounded and only just conscious, had crawled along until they were just inside the door. One of them was whimpering in a strange way. The other two were staring towards the glass chute.

Blake jumped past them and ran ahead. As he got closer to the spot he looked for Goupolis, of whom he could see no sign. Puzzled, he drew up. Had Goupolis recovered? he was asking himself. If so, where had he gone?

Then a hand gripped his shoulder and jerked him back, while he heard Tinker say:

"Back, guv'nor, back! Lookout!"

And then Blake saw the ghastly sucker end of a swaying, searching, feeling tentacle as it emerged from the broken top of the chute and probed this way and that, as if in search of something such as it had already possessed and found desirable.

He needed no more to tell him what had been the fate of Goupolis, the same to which he had sent so many victims. And, later, from the three wounded men who were almost crazed with fear, they learned that the squid had seized upon their master and dragged him through the chute before they could have helped him, had they been able.

Out in the marine-room they gazed down into the tank, where they could see the great, repulsive blotch of the squid's body high up on the side, suctioned to it, while its feeler was sent along the length of the chute. The sailors attacked it at that end with cutlasses, but it was still threshing about in awful travail hours later, until a powerful poison was poured into the tank through a hole that was smashed in the glass top.

Commander Torrini immediately took over the villa officially and, hoisting the Italian flag, established official headquarters there. He was amazed at the discovery of the big bombing aeroplane, the extraordinary wireless equipment at the room in the villa and at the tower in the village. He was astounded at the variety of mechanical gadgets which Goupolis had fixed up to control every possible source of attack, and the stupendous ingenuity that had been expended on arranging the baffling curtain maze, which, it was discovered after an exhaustive search, was controlled by a series of switches in a small room off the piazza.

But Blake was not satisfied on the latter score until he had solved the riddle of the sudden and mysterious manner in which he had lost all direction of the front door after only a couple of strides. It was simple enough in its conception. He found that the whole of the floor in the large front room, with the exception of a narrow, circular ledge that ran right round it close to the wall, was pivoted on a powerful steel rod which was operated by a clockwork mechanism that, when in motion, revolved so slowly that one standing on it was not conscious of the movement. It was sufficient, nevertheless, to carry one in a few moments well away from any given point, and that is why, after the curtains had fallen and the floor had been set in motion, Blake had lost all direction of the door. The automatics which had menaced him he also discovered later had been thrust through the curtains by Goupolis' attendants. Their soft shoes had, of course, made no sound.

But what amazed both him and the commander still, more was the appalling stock of drugs which was found only after blasting open the door of a big vault that led off the marine-room.

More than half a million pounds' worth of opium, morphine, and the various derivatives of heroin, cocaine, hedlin, medinal, and many others were found neatly packed ready for transhipment to all parts of the world. Had there been any doubt that Blake was right, it was settled then. And he knew now that he had indeed reached and smashed the very heart of the great international conspiracy that lives on lost souls.

He and Tinker rested on Mitkos for three days. They travelled in the Italian light cruiser to Port Said, where they visited Halloran once more before arranging to go to Cairo and travel by 'plane to England.

Halloran said nothing about their visit to Mitkos, but treated them in his usual casual way, offering to advance Blake what money he might need. But at that Blake smiled.

"I'll have some money from you," he said in response, "but I won't strain my credit. I'll be obliged if you will give me the value of this belt."

With that he tossed the body-belt that had stood him in such good stead on Halloran's desk.

"What's the joke?" grunted Halloran.

"No joke. What do you estimate the value?"

"About five piastres —as a souvenir."

Blake tapped one of the metal studs with which the webbing was protected.

"You'll find it's worth a bit more, Halloran. Test those studs — pure platinum,"

And Halloran's mouth dropped as he realised the simple means by which Blake had provided for necessary financial needs in case he got into a tight hole. But he never did learn of what use the detective found the oddly-fashioned buckle.

THE END.   [44900 WORDS]

A Short Complete Story.

Crooks' Cunning.

By a Popular Author.

Chapter 1   The Warning.

PIPE in mouth, attired in a comfortable walking suit of tweeds, Harry, otherwise "Bulldog" Holdfast, swung along the hedge-bordered road towards the picturesque farmhouse which had been his quarters for the past two days.

He had selected a quaint little hamlet called Penn for a short country holiday. It lay four miles from Beaconsfield and a similar distance from High Wycombe, and was an ideal spot for a real rest.

He had been out for a long tramp, and was returning for a belated tea just as the bells of a distant church chimed the hour of seven.

Holdfast suddenly heard a rush of feet around a curve in the road that hid the farmhouse from his view. The next moment he found his host. Farmer Beach, hurrying towards him with a gun gripped in his hands. At his heels were a neighbouring farmer named Joyce, and some dozen farmhands from the two men's properties.

"Hallo, Beach, what's the trouble?" Holdfast asked, as he removed his pipe from between his teeth and pulled up.

"He's been at it again, Mr. Holdfast!" answered the farmer through grating teeth; and, as he flung up a hand and pointed in the direction whence his paying guest had come, the "Bulldog" saw that his face was working with a fierce anger.

Harry Holdfast swung round and saw a cloud of smoke some quarter of a mile away in a meadow owned by the farmer.

"What is it?" he asked. "I mean what is it burning?"

"A haystack, Mr. Holdfast —but only one of a score or more some criminal or madman has deliberately destroyed in these parts during the last fortnight," was the reply. "But we can't stop, sir. Though there's not much chance of catching the hound now that he has done his work, we must at least try to get him."

The two farmers and their employees —the latter were armed with pitchforks and sticks —hurried past Holdfast, and broke through a gap in the hedge.

For just a moment Harry hesitated. Then, in his turn, he broke into a run and went after them.

They reached the haystack, and a glance told Harry that it was doomed. It must have been set afire at several points almost simultaneously, for Holdfast felt ready to wager that it had not been burning when, ten minutes ago, he had passed the vicinity in returning from his walk, and it was now hopelessly ablaze.

The farmers and farmhands separated and searched the roads near the field, but to no avail. They had fallen in with no suspicious person who might be responsible for the dastardly act.

They found Holdfast standing near the haystack, which was rapidly becoming a charred ruin. At his feet were three petrol cans, and he pointed to them meaningly.

"I found these under the hedge over there, Beach," he said. "I thought at first that it might be children with distorted ideas of a joke who had started the fire, but children would not be able to buy petrol to make sure of the hay being quickly destroyed. It's the work of someone who acted with a very grim determination. What's the idea, do you think?"

"None of us know, sir," returned Farmer Beach. "As I think I said, this sort of thing has been going on almost every night for the past two weeks, and sometimes we have found two haystacks burning at the same moment."

Holdfast whistled softly. This suggested that more than one man was responsible, so it was hardly the doing of some crank with a kink in his brain. The "Bulldog" had known important and even sinister developments come of matters that at first appeared more or less trifling, and he felt sure that he had been right in thinking that there might be far more behind this wanton damage of property than was visible upon the surface.

A little dejectedly, for his loss was no small one, Farmer Beach returned home with Holdfast; his fellow-farmer and the hands following.

When Holdfast and his host entered the scrupulously clean kitchen, where the farmer, his wife, and their guest were wont to take their meals, they found that Mrs. Beach had a visitor.

He was attired in the blue uniform of an inspector of police. He was a bearded man of forty or so, with a somewhat aggressive red face, and Farmer Beach introduced him an Inspector Jephson, of the Beaconsfield police.

"So there's been another haystack burned to-night, Beach?" the inspector said.

"Yes," answered the farmer. "I have been telling Mr. Holdfast here about the business, and"—with a glance at the "Bulldog"— "I've been hoping he might take a look into it. He has a reputation for clearing up mysteries."

"Oh, that sort of thing's the work of the police, and can be left to us!" Inspector Jephson said, with a glance at Holdfast in which there was a hint of contempt, "I don't know that we care about amateurs interfering."

Holdfast permitted himself the ghost of a smile. But he made no retort. He was wondering what had brought Inspector Jephson to the farmhouse.

He was soon to know.

The worthy official presently produced an envelope from his pocket, which Holdfast saw was addressed to Beaconsfield Police station in roughly printed characters. From it Jephson took a sheet of paper, and handed it to the farmer.

"Look at that," he said.

Holdfast saw Farmer Beach's face redden with anger as he studied the missive. The farmer passed it to his guest, and Holdfast saw that it had been crudely printed, like its covering. It ran:

"TO THE FOOLS OF POLICE. —WHAT HAS HAPPENED SO FAR HAS BEEN ONLY A PRELIMINARY CANTER. ON THE 20TH INST., BEFORE 10.30, EVERY HAYSTACK SOUTH OF PENN, AND PERHAPS A HOUSE OR TWO AS WELL, WILL BE BLAZING— YOURS,

"THE FIRE FIEND."

"The fellow must be mad," Farmer Beach declared, as Holdfast handed the communication back to the inspector. "No sane man would send a letter like that, or, for that matter, go about doing such damage."

"Oh, he's mad right enough, I fancy!" answered Jephson. "But after the twentieth —that's in three days' time —when he says he's going to give us a sort of Brock's benefit, he'll be where he can do no harm. I have arranged with Inspector Collins, of High Wycombe, to co-operate with me in the beggar's capture, and every available constable will be hidden and on the look-out for him south of Penn on the night he mentions. We shall get him as soon as he show's himself and begins operations, without the shadow of a doubt."

Holdfast still remained unusually quiet. He had his own opinions as to whether Inspector Jephson was likely to catch his man, in spite of the elaborate net he was spreading.

On the following morning Harry Holdfast paid a visit to a store in Penn's little village where petrol could be bought.

"Had they sold an unusual amount to any customer lately?" he wanted to know. "Or had they any new customer who during the last fortnight had bought a quantity of tins?"

The proprietor's, answer to both questions was in the negative, and Harry Holdfast tried several garages in Beaconsfield and the district. Here, again, he drew blank, but met with more success at High Wycombe.

The proprietor of a garage there had recently had a regular caller for petrol, whom he could not remember having served prior to about a fortnight before.

"He drives a grey racing car, sir," he informed Holdfast. "He — well, speak of angels! Here he is now!"

"Not a word about what I have been saying to you," Holdfast whispered, in a warning tone, as he slipped a ten-shilling note into the man's hand. "So this is the gentleman, is it?"

Holdfast moved from the garage, his keen eyes, upon the tall, slimly-built man, who had just pulled up outside in a rakish racing car. Next moment, as the latter turned his head and Holdfast saw his face, it was all that the "Bulldog" could do to repress a cry of surprise,

For he recognised the motorist as a crook of the "swell mobsman" type, who not long ago had been pointed out to him by his friend, Detective-sergeant Dempster, of Scotland Yard.

"By shots! Charles Carey, otherwise 'Gentleman' Charles!" he muttered, under his breath, as he strode away up High Wycombe's High Street. "Then there's something big behind it all, as I was inclined to think from the very first!"

CHAPTER 2. Rounded Up.

"DEAR old chap, —Do you feel like some excitement, and perhaps a glorious scrap? If so, meet me smoking-room, White Hart, Beaconsfield, at 9.30, on night of 20th. —HARRY HOLDFAST."

On the 19th, in other words, two days after the events narrated in our last chapter, a dozen young men in London received a copy of the above telegram.

They were mostly young fellows whom Harry Holdfast had fallen in with during the War, and a few years ago they had worn either blue or khaki with distinction and covered themselves with glory.

On the night of the 20th, without exception, they turned up at Beaconsfield, and, to their surprise, met one another either in or on their way to the White Hart Hotel.

Holdfast joined them at two minutes to the half-hour, and, without as yet explaining his real reasons for wiring them, he told them to squeeze into his car.

It meant that some had to sit on the knees of others, but they were all young fellows who found life somewhat monotonous after the excitement of the War, so that, with possible danger and a fight pending, they did not mind that.

Holdfast drove the car back towards Penn, but, skirting the hamlet, he took a road running north of it.

Presently he pulled up in a dark side road, and instructed his friends to "tumble out" and follow him.

Five minutes later he was climbing some low rails that enclosed the spacious front garden of a stately mansion.

"Couldn't go in by the drive gates, boys," he explained, in a low tone, as his friends followed him. "We might have been seen from the windows. Creep through the shrubs and hide down by the drive near the front door. We are now on the property of Colonel Sir Ian Carruthers, one of the keenest and wealthiest collectors of art treasures in England. In yonder house is a huge fortune in Old Masters, ancient armour of bronze and steel, tapestries, rare porcelain, Persian rugs, Oriental cabinets, First Empire chairs, and the like, a veritable museum of spoils of distant ages and of many lands —and we are going to stop them being stolen."

He would say no more. The party separated, and found hiding-places amongst the rhododendrons near the drive. An hour passed without anything happening, then there came a rumbling of wheels from the road, and a large pantechnicon was driven boldly into the drive and brought to a standstill, lengthwise, before the steps.

Its doors swung open, and six men sprang out. Another, who had been driving, also descended to the ground. In the moonlight Holdfast recognised him as "Gentleman" Charles, in spite of the well-worn clothes and green-baize apron in which he was clad;

Without hesitation, the crook mounted the steps and knocked and rang. A footman opened the door, and found a revolver clapped to his head.

"A sound and you're a dead man!" "Gentleman" Charles rapped.

Then he passed the terrified manservant to his companions, who quickly bound him and flung him down at the edge of the drive.

Twice more did "Gentleman" Charles tug at the bell, and a second footman and a butler who answered the ringing shared a similar fate to that which had overtaken the first servant to make his appearance. Then Colonel Sir Ian Carruthers himself came to see what all the commotion was about, and as he faced "Gentleman" Charles on the step, the latter covered him with his weapon.

"Hands up, colonel!" the crook drawled. "My friends and I have taken a fancy to your collection of art treasures and antiquities, and we are going to remove them in this van we have thoughtfully brought with us."

The colonel was a brave man, and, turning his head, he shouted to a startled maidservant, who had entered the hall to telephone for the police.

"No good, colonel," Gentleman Charles assured him. "The wires are cut; but even if they weren't, no force of police strong enough to deal with my pals and myself could be got here in time. They are all five or six miles away, looking for haystack burners who have decided to go out of the business."

He signed to two of his gang to bind the colonel. But Holdfast thought matters had gone far enough.

"At 'em, boys!" he shouted, leaping to his feet and whipping out a revolver.

A bound carried Holdfast to the drive. As "Gentleman" Charles swung round with a startled ejaculation, there were two flashes of flame and two revolver-shots which sounded almost as one. But it was the crook who dropped his weapon and reeled back, clutching at the shattered wrist, for Holdfast had fired the fraction of a moment before him.

The "Bulldog's" friends were close upon his heels, and never had a gang of criminals been so completely surprised. True, they put up something of a fight, but they were outnumbered, and it was only a matter of minutes ere they all lay at full-length upon the gravel, with the "Bulldog's" friends either sitting upon them or kneeling upon their chests.

Holdfast unbound the three servants who had been trussed up, and with the cords which had been used to make them prisoners and other lengths of rope the gang had with them, "Gentleman" Charles and his six companions were tied hand and foot.

After Holdfast had introduced himself to Colonel Sir Ian Carruthers, and the latter had warmly thanked him and his friends for their timely intervention, at Harry's instructions the crooks were bundled into the furniture-van.

"How on earth did you know what was going to happen, Harry?" asked one of the "Bulldog's" friends, in a puzzled tone. "You must have known all about this intended raid two days ago."

"Well, I began to think it was all a blind when the haystack-burners showed anxiety to direct the attention of the police upon their threatened activities on a certain night, and stated where they would be getting busy," Holdfast answered. "You see, I had seen 'Gentleman' Charles in the neighbourhood, and learned that he had recently been buying quite a lot of petrol, so that, if he was responsible for the burning of the haystacks, as seemed likely, it was plain some big criminal enterprise was in the background.

"Then suddenly I remembered reading that, three weeks ago at Christie's, Colonel Sir Ian Carruthers had bought another, famous art treasure, which he intended adding to his collection; and that it was one of the most valuable in the world. I realised that the colonel lived in the neighbourhood, and that his house stood in exactly the opposite direction to where the fire-fiends had vowed they would go to work, and I began to see daylight. The idea was, of course, to entice all the police of the district into one spot some distance removed from the colonel's house at the time when the raid was to be made. It was a clever plan to keep the police out of the way whilst the colonel's house was ransacked and the thieves got well away; but we managed to nip it in the bud. Come along, let's drive south of Penn," he added with a chuckle. "I've bet Jephson a tenner that he'd be wasting his time to-night."

Harry Holdfast mounted to the driving-seat of the pantechnicon.

With his friends riding inside with the captured thieves, he drove the cumbersome vehicle to the spot, some five miles distant, where he had last seen Inspector Jephson.

Harry Holdfast shouted, and presently the inspector bobbed up from behind a hedge. He first stared in blank surprise, as Holdfast descended from the van, then looked sheepish.

"Nothing's happened yet," he began, "but —"

"Nothing's going to happen, old top," Holdfast assured him with conviction. "By the way, I've a little present for you inside this old bus —and you owe the Beaconsfield Cottage Hospital a tenner!"

THE END.
S.S.

Our Magazine Corner
Crooks' Codes

THE amazing ingenuity which has been displayed by criminals in the organising of their coups has astounded the police time and again. The master-crook, under cover of his West-End, man-about-town role, gives his orders, and they are passed through innumerable different channels to his underlings. A gentleman in a top-hat murmurs some inconsequential remark, which cloaks an entirely different meaning, to an individual of less pretentious appearance in some West-End bar; the gentleman of less pretentious appearance strolls along the Strand and whispers something to a news-seller; the news-seller passes the word to a street hawker, and so the news spreads, and the cleverest detective in the world would find it almost impossible to trace the information —even if he were clever enough to got hold of it —to its original source.

Codes are used frequently, and a short while ago it was discovered that even a secret language had been invented and was in use among big International crooks.

A certain notorious crook, one Alberto Pinto, was arrested in Brazil, and when searched was found to have in his possession a letter written in a strange language. After very lengthy and somewhat severe interrogation, Pinto apparently admitted that the language was one introduced at an international conference of crooks held at Lorida in Spain. This language had been specially compiled so that gentlemen of the crook fraternity could communicate with each other either by letter or speech without fear of being detected by the police.

The Lorida conference was really a most ambitious movement in the criminal world. It was proposed that the various large international gangs should amalgamate into one huge organisation, with an executive committee to arrange the details of all the coups. They would also appoint the members who would carry out the job and afterwards distribute the plunder. While a copy of the language, or code, as it really is, was sent to the Director of Police at Lyons for translation into French, it is not known what was the actual outcome of the crooks' conference.

One of the greatest experts on the secret of codes and their translation, is Dr. Locard, the French detective. Among many stories told of his experiences is a case where the police discovered a code message on a suspect.

It appeared to the doctor that this was what is known as a "monoalphabetic" code, but written with a key word or phrase. After considerable effort he discovered that the code-phrase was "Paris-Lyons-Marseille," which is the name given to the railway system between Paris and the South of France. "P" represented 1, "a" stood for 2, "r" stood for 3 —and so on. When the message was deciphered, it was found that a certain well-known crook meant to rob a house in the Rue Romarin that night. It was discovered that the suspect on whom the message had been found, had visited the house earlier and had succeeded in getting wax impressions of the keyholes in order to have master keys made that would give the bigger crook easy access. That night the police hid in the shadows by the house, and when the thief put in an appearance and attempted to use his master key, they nabbed him.

Among the apaches of Paris, codes are used extensively, and many of them are amazingly ingenious. They also have a jargon which they call the "jar," and of which the average Frenchman could make nothing.

Often when a crook knows that he is about to be arrested, he will attempt to burn any incriminating papers and messages that he has, and it is here that the police are able to show that even fire does not always baffle them.

Directly the charred papers are seen, the fire is smothered. Water must not be used, as this would damage the brittle paper. The papers are then blown into the air with a fan and caught on a shoot of glass. Collodion[3] is spread gently on both sides of the paper, which is then pressed between two thin pieces of glass. In this way it can be photographed and preserved indefinitely.

---

[3] Collodion is a flammable, syrupy solution of nitrocellulose in ether and alcohol. There are two basic types: flexible and non-flexible. The flexible type is often used as a surgical dressing or to hold dressings in place. When painted on the skin, collodion dries to form a flexible nitrocellulose film.

www.ingramcontent.com/pod-product-compliance
Lightning Source LLC
Chambersburg PA
CBHW051851170626
46807CB00003B/1428